Three rode the path together,
yet they were not alone . . .

COMPANIONS ON THE ROAD

The citadel of Avillis had burned through the night with its terrible Lord and his monstrous children in it. Nothing remained now but waste, ruin, and, at the heart of the palace, the great cup of Avillis, still untouched.

Untouched until borne away by Kachil, Feluce, and Havor. All too soon they would taste of unquenchable fear, unknowable Fate . . . and of the essense of the Chalice that, once stolen, could not be lightly cast aside, even in horror and despair.

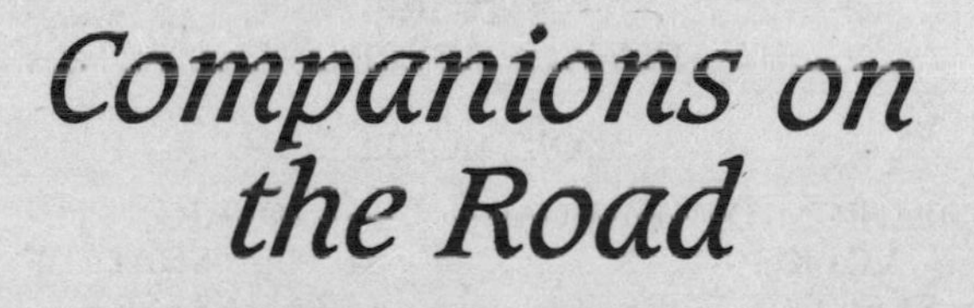

DAW Books presents
classic works of imaginative fiction
by multiple award-winning author
TANITH LEE

THE BIRTHGRAVE TRILOGY

THE BIRTHGRAVE
SHADOWFIRE
(originally published as *Vazkor, Son of Vazkor*)
HUNTING THE WHITE WITCH
(originally published as *Quest for the White Witch*)

TALES FROM THE FLAT EARTH

NIGHT'S MASTER
DEATH'S MASTER
DELUSION'S MASTER
DELIRIUM'S MISTRESS
NIGHT'S SORCERIES

THE WARS OF VIS

THE STORM LORD
ANACKIRE
THE WHITE SERPENT

AND MORE:

COMPANIONS ON THE ROAD
VOLKHAVAAR
ELECTRIC FOREST
SABELLA
KILL THE DEAD
DAY BY NIGHT
LYCANTHIA
DARK CASTLE, WHITE HORSE
CYRION
SUNG IN SHADOW
TAMASTARA
THE GORGON AND OTHER BEASTLY TALES
DAYS OF GRASS
A HEROINE OF THE WORLD
REDDER THAN BLOOD

DAW is proud to be reissuing these classic books in new editions beginning in 2015.

Companions on the Road

TANITH LEE

DAW BOOKS, INC.
DONALD A. WOLLHEIM, FOUNDER
375 Hudson Street, New York, NY 10014
ELIZABETH R. WOLLHEIM
SHEILA E. GILBERT
PUBLISHERS
www.dawbooks.com

Cover art by Bastien Lecouffe Deharme.

Cover design by G-Force Design.

DAW Book Collectors No. 1791.

Published by DAW Books, Inc.
375 Hudson Street, New York, NY 10014.

First DAW Printing, June 2018

1 2 3 4 5 6 7 8 9

DAW TRADEMARK REGISTERED
U.S. PAT. AND TM. OFF. AND FOREIGN COUNTRIES
—MARCA REGISTRADA
HECHO EN U.S.A.

PRINTED IN THE U.S.A.

Table of Contents

COMPANIONS ON THE ROAD

1. Avillis 3
2. The Chalice 17
3. Supper at Axa 25
4. The Road 43
5. Night 53
6. Afternoon in Arnos 61
7. The Snow-Waste 73
8. Silsi 89
9. The Dark 97

THE WINTER PLAYERS

1. Sea Grey 113
2. Grey Wolf's Running 127
3. Red Ship 143
4. Land of White Swords 157
5. Black Room, Black Road 169
6. Blue Cave 183
7. Sea Blue 199

Companions on the Road

1. Avillis

THE NIGHT THEY TOOK AVILLIS was a night of blood, and blood-red flame.

It was the last city this side of the Great River, the end of the King's long autumn campaign. The trees were already stripped black and bare as old bones when the troops came marching from the South, the skies white with snow-waiting. The King and his captains had expected a long siege, and there had been a deal of unease among the men, the soldiers squatting by their fires, the officers talking too loudly round their wine in the tents. For a certain thing had been said all along the muddy tracks and the broken roads, said more softly, yet more insistently, as city after city fell to the King, and the embattled lines moved farther and farther North.

That night, the night Avillis was to fall, this certain thing swirled and breathed about the camp like fog. For the Lord of Avillis, so it was said, was in league with the Powers of the Dark.

Havor of Taon was sitting at his own fire when the early dusk came down. It was the second day of the siege, and, like the rest of them, he expected it to be a long one.

There was a weary sense of unfulfillment on him that twilight that had something to do with the dreariness of the coming winter, but was mostly his own disillusion with the King's war, which he had fought for two years.

Havor was an outlander from the far North beyond the Great River, tall, slender, long of leg and pitch-black of hair, with the orange-brown eyes of a hawk which had acquired for him the relevant nickname among his soldiers. For, though younger than most, he had earned himself a command on the autumn campaign, albeit a small one. Now, at eighteen, he wore the badge of the King's Bear, and was a captain of thirty men. For anyone who had wanted to make a career for himself in the King's armies, that was a fair start. All in all he had not done badly out of the war, but the smells of it, the sights of it, and the cries of pain that attended it like the vultures, had sickened and soured him. Yes, he could fight well enough. And kill efficiently. He feared death, like other men, but could put that from his mind in battle, and he was no fool with a sword or knife. But several smoking ruins ago there had come a curious shift inside himself. He had lost his sense of purpose in the war; he supposed because it was not truly his own purpose but that of the King.

His kin were long since dead; he had scarcely known them. There had been a plague, so people had told him after, and soon he was an orphan, to be brought up in one of the great religious hostels of those lands. There had been little kindness in that place, asprawl with homeless children, and no love. When he was ten he had run from it, and since then made his own way in the world. He had been merchant's boy, and baker's boy, blown bellows for a blacksmith, crossed the River and rigged sails, sold horses in the markets to the East, grown older, learned a little, hardened a little, been recruited at last to the King's army in the summer drought three years before because the King's propaganda had promised each man a stoup of water both morning and night—which had been, as it turned out, a lie.

He was going over all this, his past, outside besieged Avillis on that night of whispers.

A little way down, in a hollow among some trees, his men were cursing and laughing over their beer, but their laughter had a strange, false note to it.

"Well," said someone from behind, "what a broody hawk you are tonight, Havor."

It was a light, pleasing voice, but it did not please Havor. Feluce, his Second—though not appointed by him—had stolen up like a shadow. His tone was, as always, derisively polite. Feluce was the son of a Southern cloth-vendor, anxious at all times to appear better than he was, as he judged better to be. He came round the fire to face Havor, and stood smiling, his thumbs hooked in his belt, elegant, handsome, snow-blond and unspeakably arrogant. He produced in Havor an anger as bitter and enduring as it was without apparent reason. But it was an anger he never showed, and he sensed that Feluce, trying always to goad him, found this frustrating.

"Well," Feluce said again, "have you heard the latest tale about the Lord of Avillis? Apparently he shape-changed into a black cloud and flew off across the setting sun. At least a hundred men will swear to having seen it, and make the sign of the holy circle to protect themselves while they're telling you."

"No, I hadn't heard that."

"Oh, well, it's been nothing but stories and nightmares for twenty miles back. Blood sacrifices to the Forces of Evil—the Lord is the Arch Magus, seemingly, his son a warlock, his daughter a sorceress. They say she has golden hair," Feluce remarked. He took a certain pride in his way with girls. "At any rate, a family so well-loved by devils and demons should make light of escaping our paltry little siege, should it not?"

"I've heard the Lord and his children are hated in Avillis," said another voice.

Havor did not need to turn; he was good at voices. This one belonged to Lukon, a boy also from his own command, a very young boy, an obedient soldier on the march, as yet untried in the war. This last battle, if it came, would be his first.

"Ah, here's the baby," Feluce said. He always called Lukon this, sweetly, and Lukon, locked by the discipline of his rank, would redden with a painful suppressed hurt and fury.

"Feluce," Havor said quietly, "go and see if the men got their rations, will you? There was some bother earlier."

Feluce laughed in a melodious, soft way he had, and bowed like an actor before turning and nonchalantly idling off, roughly in the direction of the hollow. It was only an excuse and he knew it. Havor had sensed in Lukon a bewildered fear, a need to speak. Yet it had always been difficult to give an order to Feluce and at the same time prevent bickering.

"Sit down if you want," Havor said to the boy. "Have you eaten?"

Lukon sat opposite to him, across the weary little blaze. Overhead, stark white winter stars were coming out. The camp, the great walls half a mile ahead, had been reduced to an amalgamated blur by the thickening dusk, picked out only here and there by the red chalks of the fires.

"I—didn't feel much like eating, sir."

Havor tossed a leather flask across to the boy.

"Here. Drink some of this."

The boy gulped with an embarrassed gratitude, and

Havor wondered at himself. He thought: In a week, a month—whenever the siege breaks and the troops disband—I shall ride away from this life and its responsibilities, and then there'll be no more Lukons trying to explain their terrors to me across a fire.

Then Lukon surprised him.

"Sir, I've not been with the army for long—but—can I ask you for a favor—a special favor?"

"What is it?"

"It's my family, sir, my mother, and my two sisters. We've got a farm southwest from here, a little way from Venca. It's not good land. I said I'd try to save some of my pay to send them. And well . . . if anything—if there's a fight for Avillis, and I. . . . Can you get this to them?"

He held out to Havor a small cloth bag that gave off a little clinking sound, as if Lukon's hand was trembling. Havor sat still, not taking the bag. The boy's trust moved him, disorganized him.

"I know it's a deal to ask," Lukon said, the bag wavering now.

"Lukon," Havor said slowly, "how do you know I won't keep this money for myself, whether you live or die?"

"Oh, no, sir. You wouldn't do that."

Havor smiled wryly.

"Is my honesty so transparent?" He reached and took the bag. "All right. Don't fret. I'll keep it for you till our King has Avillis. Then I'll give it you again and you can take it to your mother yourself."

Lukon stood up. He said very gravely, "Thank you, sir. There's an old road runs near—you'd know the house by a great crippled pine on the west side." Then he relaxed a little, and added, half embarrassed again, "I can sleep easier now. So, if you don't mind, sir, they're grilling fish down there, and my appetite seems to have come back. . . ."

Odd, how different different men's fears could be.

Later, Havor rolled himself in his blanket under the stars and let the fire drowse him. He anticipated no danger or event of that night. As he slipped into sleep he heard a wolf howl, far off somewhere in the black bone woods—the first wolf of the winter.

Half a minute later, it seemed, a man was shaking his shoulder.

"Camp alert, captain. Rouse your men."

Havor stared around through the moonlit night. The wind smelled of smoke and urgency.

"What is it? Are they attacking us?"

"No." The man grinned. "We them. The city hates its Lord and won't suffer siege for him. Some traitor's opened the gates and given us a signal."

"It may be a trap."

"The King doesn't think so."

And the man moved off about his shaking-waking work.

Havor got his men awake; while they were ordering and arming themselves and kicking dirt over their fires, Havor stood on the ridge, observing the camp. Preparation for battle was a familiar sight, yet this night made unfamiliar and stealthy by the dark and the need for deception. Horses stamped, smokes blew. Here and there came the monotonous bees-droning of the four or five camp priests hastily shriving those who asked for it. Havor's men, on the whole, were an irreligious lot. Only Lukon had slipped off, and was shortly back with that curious look of having been comforted that Havor could not understand. He had been too near the hard facts of religion as a child to find it soothing. The priests had beaten him and starved him, and so that was what he associated with the holy circle of eternal life.

Half an hour later they were riding soft up the sere grassy hillocks to the city's Goat Gate, that drovers' entry now left unbarred for them. Men slunk ahead to deal with possible sentries, slipped in and out again, reporting that the watch seemed to have deserted and that nothing moved on the streets but rats, for it was the slum-quarter they would be entering.

For Havor, that entry had a dreamlike, macabre quality. So dark, so silent, the great mass crept in at the narrow gate, only three riders at a time, to be greeted by the darkness and silence of hovels and alleys where they must split into companies and ride single file. No one peered out at them, not a light showed. They surely knew in there what moved in Avillis. Was it the hatred of their Lord, the Magus, or only terror of the invader that kept them so still?

It was nearly midnight. The black quiet and the stealth began to oppress him, but action came presently.

The streets broadened. Among the mansions of Avillis the war cry rose and spread, torchlight burst yellow and red and leaped to embrace the city and the sky. Havor saw the first house catch ablaze, the embroidery of the flame, the struts standing out like bones on the bright core within, while human ants came scurrying out from it. Avillis was the last city of the campaign and the most insolent. The King, Havor knew, reckoned on his own brand of justice. Avillis would be sacked and razed, and no quarter given. That she had betrayed herself to him would only make his hand heavier. The King hated treachery, so he said, though it had helped him often enough in his war.

As the dark bled into carmine, the confusion of battle overcame Havor. The winding streets were alive with flame and screaming. Afterwards he had only dim memories, fire-edged but inconclusive, of galloping up the sloping avenues toward the citadel. They took the garrison, caught slovenly and unawares, sword met sword with a dull and brutal clangor, and here too, the black night was exchanged for scarlet and the whirling of sparks.

The soldiers, so uneasy before, now vented their fear in violence. Finding nothing important opposed them, they whipped Avillis as they would have done in their villages the charlatan who had claimed to be a witch. The citadel, crouching like a black animal atop Avillis, cracked suddenly on fire, plumes of smoke erupting into the purple winter sky.

Havor found himself alone in the rabid shadows, trying to ease the excited horse, his sword too red in the flame-glare. All around men ran hooting, and somewhere frenzied bells were tolling. Up there, the palace of the Lord of Avillis burned.

He watched it to the end, wondering vaguely if the Lord, his son and his daughter had surrendered themselves to the King. Strangely, he felt a conviction that they had not. That was their funeral pyre, then, that flaring mound which gradually sank down into itself, leaving only a ruined lacework of blackened stone to filter the promise of dawn which finally drained the fires from Avillis.

He walked the horse back along the streets in that sheeny lightening that heightens the sky and bleaches the landscape long before the first finger of dawn sifts the horizon. The city was horrible, now that the abstract glory of the fire had left it. On every side soldiers were looting the houses: they seemed the only live things remaining in Avillis, which had been left a ragged corpse to face the sunrise.

Once or twice there was trouble—some man who had

not had enough, still looking for a fight, but they were mostly stupid with wine, and easily dealt with. In an alley he found a soldier tearing the earrings off the ears of a crippled girl, and clouted him insensible. The girl limped away immediately. It seemed to Havor a pointless rescue. All over the city similar things—or worse—were happening, and he could not be everywhere.

On a certain street, great heaps of velvets and furs were being loaded on to a wagon. Inside the despoiled mansion Havor resigned his captaincy and badge of office with its bear symbol to a swearing, blue-jowled commander with his leg upon a smoke-stained stool. The commander interspersed his jokes at Havor's expense with oaths directed at the surgeon attending him.

Havor came out, a taste of salt in his mouth, stripped of so very little, yet, oddly, so much. His war gear was his own—the King's armies were not overgenerous when supplying the lower ranks of the soldiers—the sword, and the black horse with the dun mane, too: a good horse, and a good blade, for he had learned horses and metal long ago. Yet the rest of his two years life was suddenly gone from him. And, although the decision had been made long since, he felt himself bewildered, at a loss; most of all, dog-tired.

Ashes blew on the wind.

There was a little wine-shop on a corner. The door was hanging loose but the place was lit and crammed by the King's troops, rowdy with the stolen liquor. A group of soldiers—Havor recognized them vaguely as some of his own—were lounging about the doorposts where the saffron glare spilled out, watching a young Second with white-fair hair tip the drink into his upturned mouth with self-conscious yet elegant skill.

One or two men glanced up, caught sight of Havor, and saluted him awkwardly, perhaps noting the badge of the King's Bear was gone from his left shoulder. Feluce, lowering the wine-skin, half turned and laughed.

"Well, if it isn't the Hawk of Taon—our gallant captain. Come and join our victorious merry-making, Havor."

"Is Lukon with you?" Havor said.

"Lukon? Not he." Feluce grinned. "Has any one of us seen the baby? Or is he still too young to risk this chill morning air?"

A couple of them laughed too. Feluce had a certain cruel charm that caught some hard and held them. They admired his looks, his vicious sweet-talking, the barbed tongue that passed for wit.

But there was a man on the edge of the group with a bandage tied round his head. He shuffled his feet and looked at Havor, without quite meeting his eyes.

"He's out of the air, all right, captain. He's with the others just outside the east wall where they're digging the burial pits. And I don't think he'll get any older now, Second Feluce, nor that you've any call to jeer at the dead."

A little silence went round the group. It was unlucky, even now, to speak of death.

"Ah!" Feluce spat. "Make the holy circle over yourself somewhere else. You're alive, aren't you, clod?"

Havor began to lead the horse away, up the street. Somewhere a bell was tolling dismally in the eastern quarter of the ruined city.

So Lukon was dead, after all. Had he guessed Avillis would have him, coming with that small bag of coins, setting this bond on a man he did not know? Havor touched the bag in his belt. Well, at least he knew his road now, for a time. A black and bitter road, with black and bitter news to tell at the end of it, and others' grief that he must witness. Because he had said he would.

Near the street's head, he found Feluce had caught up to him and was strolling at his side, smiling.

"What now, Havor? Winter at the King's capital, or adventures on the road? I see you lost the Bear."

Havor said nothing. He cursed Feluce and wished him forty miles off, but his dark Northern face and russet-gold eyes gave away none of that, only the old unreadable solitude that was always there on him, like a smoky branding.

At that moment they turned the street corner, Feluce drinking from the tilted wine-skin, Havor walking the black horse. And ahead, at the end of a brief avenue, loomed the stone banks of the citadel, black now on the raw blue-white sky, and above, the charcoal blooms still softly uncurling over what had once been the palace of Avillis.

"Did you hear?" Feluce said. "The Magus and his kin refused to be our King's prisoners. They stayed in their nest, and the fire had them."

Just then a man came darting out of a doorway.

It was sudden, unexpected. He thudded into Havor, his arm striking at Feluce, as it seemed involuntarily. Havor's hand was already loosening the knife—he anticipated trouble, and caught only a glimpse of Southern mail, a bronze-red mane, a foxy, narrow-eyed face. Then the man, drawing back, called an apology and ran on up the avenue towards the huge gate.

Havor in his weariness was astounded, momentarily unthinking. But Feluce, alert to villainy because it was so close to him, snarled, "Hell strike the devil—he's got my wages!"

Havor slid his hand along his belt and found the little cloth bag had gone too. Lukon's savings. All that was left to the poor farm near Venca to sugar their grief. A white fury rushed up his throat and sank again, dazzling him.

"Thought we were drunkards, no doubt," Feluce grated. "Quick, Taon Hawk, let's see this brute of yours catch a thief."

The bizarre happening had made bizarre comrades of

them. Havor mounted the horse, Feluce springing up behind, kicking its sides. Abruptly they were under the dark cold shadow of the gate, abruptly out of it, taking the terrace-steps of the wall three at a leap, and then found themselves on the wall's broad back, among the high ruins and the wide, lightening sky.

"There goes the scum!" Feluce kicked harder at the horse.

But the man ran fast, thin and quick on his feet, well used, perhaps, to being hunted.

There was a breach in the wall—the fox thief dropped swiftly away and down. The horse, plunging after, burst all at once into a nightmare garden where every shrub and tree had been twisted and wrenched by flame into a black skeleton.

Feluce slid clear of the animal, and pounced suddenly into those ebony bones. He and the red man came out rolling, a fume of black dust swirling up around them. Then Feluce had the soldier pinned, his knife held across his throat.

The red man lay very still. His eyes flicked to Havor.

"He's your captain—isn't him?" he said to Feluce from the side of his fox's mouth. "You're not going to kill me without he says so? Are you?"

Feluce hit him in the face.

"Filthy little street robber! Where did you put my coins?"

"There, sir, in my belt."

Feluce tore out the two money bags, one small, the other rather larger and heavier. Feluce had always seemed to carry more coins than other Seconds. No doubt he had his own methods of robbery, more subtle than the fox's. With a sensation of burning and dust in his throat, Havor felt an intense desire to turn thief also and take that larger bag, not the other, to Lukon's kin.

"You understand, sir," the foxy man was rattling on nervously, "I never ever really meant to snatch 'em—it's sort of got to be like a habit with me—"

"I'll allow you one prayer," Feluce said. "Then I'll slit your worthless throat."

"Wait!"

"Why should I? One prayer, I said."

"I'll trade you—trade you my life—for—for something I know. About this place."

Feluce smiled. "What could you possibly know about anything?"

"It's true—I swear it—there's treasure here in the Lord's palace."

"No doubt. Or was. And all scoured out now, or burned to a frazzle."

The red man's eyes glittered.

"No. There's secret rooms—*under* the palace. I know how to get in—I heard about it, months ago, three cities back—an old man at an inn, half crazy, but he had a map of the way. Let me go, my lord, and I'll show you."

Feluce glanced up at Havor. "What do you think, heroic captain?"

"I think he'll say anything to save his life," Havor said, dismounting, "which you've no right to take, in any case." He bent and scooped up the cloth bag, then swiftly struck Feluce's knife clear of the man's throat. Feluce hissed his anger like a cat.

In a moment the red-haired man had wriggled free, and was on his feet. But he did not run away.

"Fair's fair," he said modestly, conscious of his nobility. "I'll keep my word. Kachil's my name, sirs. And I'll be glad enough of company in there, for all it's coming on for daybreak."

2. The Chalice

HE SEEMED ON THE WHOLE an innocent villain, this Kachil. He baffled Havor, as did the dark windings of the gutted palace, which here and there, unexpectedly, gave way to great slabs of silver sky.

Havor's head rang from fatigue and past anger. For he was no longer angry now. A hard clenching determination had grown up in him outside, as he tethered the horse in the wild garden. He too would loot and thieve, become a sacker and despoiler of the dead. He would take what he could find, and use that to swell Lukon's cloth bag, and use it, too, to ease the telling of the cruel news at Venca, and not only for the boy's mother and sisters, but for the teller also. For himself he thought to take nothing; it did not occur to him. Wealth, or large amounts of possessions seemed to him limiting. They brought their own prison with them. He preferred, since he had once known a kind of prison, to travel free.

They reached the depths of the palace. Everything was unrecognizable. Overhead, a tangle of black galleries against the light.

Kachil led them through a jagged hole, once a doorway, and farther down, and they passed from the gloom to a second night.

"Hey you, snatch-purse," Feluce called. "Don't think you can trick me down here in the dark."

"Patience, my lord, I brought a little tallow. One moment."

A flint struck and, presently, flickering pale yellow outlined their faces. A velvet curtain, black and soft as a raven's back, hung in tatters across their path. Kachil pushed it aside, and they went on.

The corridor twisted, and seemed to run deep. Havor began to sense the pile of the broken palace, the heavy earth itself balanced over their skulls. There was no sound in that place except the sounds they themselves made—breathing, footfalls, the faint popping of the wax. And all these sounds seemed strangely muffled and deadened, as if fragments of the velvet curtain had come flapping into their ears, like invisible bats.

Kachil did not appear to like the quiet. His eyes darted and the candle trembled. Feluce seemed taut as a harpstring, vibrating with his own tension. After a moment he snarled, "This gutter-object doesn't know what he's at. He's lost us."

"No indeed, my lord. The map—the map had it that the passage turns, and there's a hidden room—"

"If it's hidden, how shall we see it, straw-brain? Or do you have the witch-sight?"

Just then they reached a sharply-angled turning, and beyond, a black bare wall.

"Ha!" Feluce gave a shout of scorn, too loud in the dead air. "Well, well. It will be down here, after all, that I end your miserable life."

"What are those markings on the wall?" Havor said. He saw the shapes of strange beasts and symbols cut into the stone, and magnified, distorted, by the burning wax and his tiredness, they seemed to coil about each other, to flash and darken and change shape.

"The way in," Kachil said breathlessly, "or should be. Now. If I press here. And here."

There came a harsh rustling, a grazing of stone on stone.

"And now—*there!*" Kachil cried softly, and with triumph.

Like a trick of the eyes or of the wavering light, the blank wall divided and altered into an oblong of darkness.

Feluce swore under his breath.

"So he was clever, too, the Magus-Lord of Avillis!"

Havor saw Kachil's hand flick up and draw the holy sign of the circle in the air, a look of brief fright on his fox face. Feluce laughed, and poked him forward with his candle, into the gaping way.

"Wait," Havor said. "Once we're inside, does the door stay open?"

"Yes, sir. Till the markings are pressed again. So the old man's map said, and it's right so far."

"This old man," Feluce said, stepping through into the place beyond the wall, "why did he never come here himself, when the Lord and his son and golden-haired daughter were busy elsewhere?"

Kachil grinned, a scared grin made demoniacal by the up-cast light of the candle. His voice came, dry and whispering. "Perhaps he did. I said he was half-crazy. It was here—here in this room—that they conjured up the Powers of the Dark, and made their offerings to Hell."

"A wonder they didn't run here then, to hide, when the King came."

Havor, the last to step inside the room, felt a thick

coldness, dank as stagnant water, wash over and envelop him. A cold common to all rooms far beneath the ground, he supposed.

Feluce snatched the tallow and lifted it.

The whole of the chamber was caught in a swinging yellow arc. It was composed of ancient stone and was quite empty of everything but shadows. Then one shadow stirred, very faintly.

Kachil whimpered; Feluce sprang backwards, then gave a raucous laugh. "A black curtain, the same as outside." Holding the smoking candle high, he strode to it. "So we came all this trek for a piece of mildewed velvet, you addled oaf." He wrenched at the curtain and brought it down—and caught his breath like a drowning man.

There was a scarlet cloth hanging on the wall, embroidered with those beasts and symbols cut into the stone outside, in silks of twenty fiery shades of green, blue, saffron and purple. Below stood a marble block, cold white, stained in places black.

Havor felt his heart swell with one huge, painful surge.

On the block stood one thing only: a Chalice, the height of a child of three or four years, made of pure gold.

The workmanship was alien and ancient, very ancient, perhaps of another time or even another earth, its sinuous coils, which seemed like serpents without heads, twisted and coaxed out beneath another sun, its scallopings and smooth leaves beaten to the tempo of another world's winds.

Set into the gold were gems, gems like the bluest of sapphires, the darkest of diamonds, rubies which were blood, topaz which were sulfurous flame. The light of the candle wheeled and broke like the sea on the Chalice, eddied and slid into its yellow fire, returned in wild refractions from every facet and every searing jewel.

Suddenly Kachil began to caper. "Didn't I say? Didn't I say!"

"A fortune," Feluce breathed. "For any man. Even for three."

Havor drew his sword. It made a rasping, hoarse noise in the cold room.

Kachil spun about, horrified.

"Do *you* mean to kill me now?"

"No," Havor said, "to save your skin. Also yours, Feluce, and mine. You see the holy circle marked on the hilt? Put both your hands on it, as I will, and swear to split the prize evenly, or not at all. Each man to give up any hopes of stealing it from the other two, or murdering the other two. Till we are rid of that thing, and have it as coins in our pockets, we are to be brothers, we three."

Feluce smiled. "Oh, the stern hawk. You're no longer my captain, Havor."

"So you stab me in my sleep at some inn," said Havor, "or I you. Or both of us Kachil. Or Kachil both of us?"

Kachil said, observing Feluce with a practiced wary eye, "I'll swear. There's my hand. It's only wise. And we'll need to stick together, perhaps, if others come sniffing after."

Havor placed his hand on Kachil's, on the engraved circle.

"Now you, Feluce," he said.

"And what about you, Northerner? I know you set no store by such things as holy circles. How do we trust your oath?"

"Because I shall keep it, whatever it's sworn by. I can give you no better answer."

Feluce was angry, but he sensed the mood of the other two, and gave in to it. He brought his hand over Havor's and swore to the bond. And Havor swore to it also. It was a flimsy surety, he thought, yet better than nothing. His eyes slipped to the golden glory. He thought abruptly, without reason, since it was so obvious: There is death in that thing if we're not careful. But there was a compulsion now, above and beyond the wage he wanted to take to Venca. Above and beyond the gold, too. Beautiful, it was so beautiful. He wanted to touch its coiling shape, the gold petals, dip his fingers into the hard light of its jewels—

He sheathed the sword, and went to the great Cup, and lifted it down. Despite its size and solidity, curiously, it was not heavy. A girl might have lifted it. Perhaps, he thought, one had.

He turned and looked back at Feluce, at Kachil, beyond them, at the door. Then he walked by them and out, and Feluce and Kachil followed him, tamely and unspeaking, their eyes fixed, as were his, only on the Chalice.

Outside it was a pale, cold day.

There was a leather sack tied to Havor's saddle, used for carrying food, flints, oddments of gear. They put the Chalice into it, and stuffed things back in along the sides to make the bag bulge in an uninteresting and ordinary way.

Havor led the horse, Kachil walked along one side of it, Feluce behind.

They went back to the wine shop where Feluce had stabled his own mount, a roan. The noise and light had died out of the place, and soldiers were snoring in the open court. Kachil had had no horse, but after a while he slipped aside and returned with one from somewhere, a docile mare, clearly not his own. He also seemed a money pouch or two heavier since they had left the wine-shop.

There was a block road that led from Avillis southwest through a scatter of towns and villages, all once in the thrall of the city, now, by right of conquest, the King's. Beyond these the road swung full west towards Venca, where there were many dealers in gold and precious stones.

"A good route to travel," said Kachil, "with the bulk of the army journeying south to the capital. We shan't want too much company on our way."

Havor seconded Kachil's choice, thinking of the farm.

They ate bread and dried meat outside the walls of Avillis. The road began by the West Gate where battered iron portals were still firm closed. A grove of tall, crow-black trees in stubborn winter leaf marked the road's beginning and stood at intervals along it, marching like sentinels by the meanderings of the ancient paving across the desolate, many-ridged landscape, away into a grey-blue smoke of distance.

The hooves of the horses struck a dull metallic noise from the blocks. A little moss had seeped up between them, but not much. The road was very old.

Overhead, the lemon smudge of sun climbed the arch of the sky as they rode from Avillis.

3. Supper at Axa

THE SUN WAS LOW AGAIN soon enough, the afternoon light condensing. They had ridden alone during their three hours journeying; no talkative, cursing soldiers seemed to be dragging their gear and spoils this way homewards, with still-sharp eyes and greedy, cunning fingers. Neither had there been any other travellers. They had met no one.

On either side now the ground sloped away steeply into the tangle of pared winter woods, with here and there one of the solitary dark-leafed trees standing straight as a candle flame. Beyond the woods rolled the static faint blue waves of distant hills. It was very quiet, and the horses' hooves rang loud on the road. Once a large black bird rose silent and soaring from the trees on ragged wings. It was all the life they saw.

"You said you knew this road, thief," Feluce remarked to Kachil. "Is there an inn or a town to give us shelter and entertainment for the night?"

"I've never come this way myself," Kachil said hastily, "but I heard there's a town a mile or so farther on—Axa. And there's an inn."

Feluce yawned. "Some scruffy place, no doubt, that serves boiled rats'-meat for stew."

Since they had been on the road, carrying the Cup, Feluce had become more haughty and mannered than ever before. Now his eyes slid to the leather sack tied to Havor's saddle.

"Do you have it safe, noble captain?"

"It's safe."

Havor's weariness had fined down into a bright, tight, weightless state. The road and the sky glared, both the same throbbing shade of white. All movement seemed silver-etched on the air so that it left a mark behind it in space, and for an hour now he had been aware of the recurring bronze scoring that was Kachil's head turning to look apprehensively over its shoulder. Feluce had apparently begun to notice it too.

"Fearful of pursuit, thief-friend?"

"We don't want to be crowded, sir, do we?" Kachil said. He was obviously still afraid of Feluce. "I was just keeping a look-out." He paused and added uncertainly, "It seems to me there are some riders back there, a couple of miles behind. I reckoned so for about an hour now, but I can't be sure . . ."

Feluce glanced over his shoulder also.

"Nothing there, red thief. Your eyes are playing tricks."

"That's odd. I could have sworn—"

"Here, Havor. What do you say? How about exercising that hawk-sight, and settling the dispute?"

Havor noted that Kachil appeared ill at ease, fiddling with the reins of his stolen horse; Feluce's disdain seemed an attempt to mask some other emotion.

Turning a little in his saddle, Havor looked back along the road.

For a long stretch it was empty of everything, curving and bare as a pale serpent. Yet far off, distant as the edge of vision, something moved. At first he could not be sure, he seemed to be staring after a reflection on water, or a cloud, a thing that lost its shape, altered itself, became another thing.

"Is it soldiers?" Kachil asked.

"No," Havor said softly, "three dark riders, one with a yellow hood."

He looked away from the road, back at the two beside him. Feluce yawned again, too extravagantly. Kachil gnawed his mouth.

"Who could they be?"

"Priests, perhaps," Feluce sneered, "and we can all make confession of our sins at this flea-ridden town we're about to surprise with our custom."

He lifted his head and began to sing, some roundelay of the South. He had a good voice, and knew it, yet, perhaps because of the cold, the notes came harsh today.

They rode on along the old road.

The sun was burning out like a furnace behind the trees, when the walls of Axa appeared on the road crest ahead of them. Stout walls they were, of dark red stone, with two or three reddish narrow towers and many slanting roofs poking above them.

They had not been over-hasty; night was flooding the sky and there were men by the gate-house, ready to close the town gates. They let the three mailed riders pass through, but cast uneasy glances after their Southern mail.

"You there!" Feluce called out, like a lord. "Where's the nearest reasonable inn?"

The men exchanged looks. One said respectfully, carefully, "You could try the Black Bird—go left, there, then up Chicken Street . . ." He faltered, then added, "Do you come from Avillis, sir?"

"Avillis?" Feluce looked puzzled. *"Avillis?* There's a pile of ruins, still smoking, some miles back along the road. Would that be Avillis?"

The man's face paled. His hand flew up to draw the shape of the holy circle.

"And the Lord of Avillis?" he presently asked.

"Burned to a cinder. The son and the pretty witch-daughter, too."

With a cheerful mocking salute, Feluce swung his horse about, and they rode off, leaving the man standing very still in the darkening street.

As they clattered up close-packed alleys, the upper galleries of houses leaning near together as gossips over their heads, Kachil whined, "You shouldn't have boasted about it, sir—you shouldn't have—"

"Ah, hold your tongue, you brainless eel. They'll know, like all the rest, what our King does to towns that molest his soldiers. We'll be treated very well here. Besides, the fools feared that Lord of theirs, you could see it in their eyes. Eh, Havor?"

"So it would seem."

Kachil muttered to himself. He was shivering, his teeth chattering, yet there was high color in his narrow face. A racking chill had come on him an hour before, making him crochety and anxious. Abruptly he gave a thin little chuckle.

"What tickles *you,* clown?" snapped Feluce.

"Those others, those other riders—by the time they reach the town the gates will be shut."

A moon had appeared on the purple strip of sky between the roof tops overhead. They reached the end of Chicken Street, and found the inn, a sprawling house with bulging windows reddish from internal firelight. Above the lintel swung a big old brass cage with a crow in it, shiny-black as oil and with a single hard glass-bright eye. It was pecking up scraps of bloody meat, but when it saw them it uttered a raucous lament and hopped to the bars, thrusting out its head and wicked beak, staring at them from its one eye.

Feluce laughed. Standing in the stirrups he reached up and flipped with the pommel of his knife, setting the cage swinging. The crow slithered, its claws scratching frantically, and began to screech.

A man came hurrying from inside, and stopped short when he saw them. He had a broad leathery face, a thickly-veined nose. His eyes hurried over their mail.

"My lords . . . ?"

"We're the King's men," Feluce said, grinning. "We want the best supper your poverty-stricken kitchen can offer us, the pick of your no doubt vile wines, and well-aired beds, probably with well-aired fleas in them."

"This is a clean house, sir."

"Oh, don't stand on your dignity with me, landlord. Send a boy to stable our horses, and get some ale heated."

The inn-keeper went inside with a blank face. Kachil giggled and shivered. A boy ran out and took their animals as they dismounted.

"I expect them with burnished coats and full bellies in the morning," Feluce flung after him.

Inside, the inn was ambered with firelight from a great hearth, and a blonde girl was lighting candles in wax-tasselled sconces. Here and there at the trestles and around the fire sat a few customers, not travellers but local men from the look of them. There was an air of much noise cut suddenly off. Eyes stared and mouths tightened.

Feluce swaggered to the hearth and glanced disdainfully about at the group already seated there, an elegant hand resting casually on his sword hilt. One by one, without a murmur, the men got up and moved back, leaving the fire to him and his companions.

Feluce looked at Havor. "Does my conduct offend you? I'm heartily sorry. Did you bring in our keepsake?"

Havor placed the leather sack with other items of gear on the bench by Feluce, unspeaking.

Kachil looked at the sack and giggled again. *"I'll take my wine in a golden cup,"* he warbled.

Feluce pushed him into a chair. "Shut up, fool! Are we to have no peace from your infernal idiocy?"

"Let him alone," Havor said quietly. "He's sick."

"And he makes me sick with his stupidity." Feluce turned, and shouted at the girl for the ale he had ordered, so that she fled with wide eyes for the door.

There was no sound in the taproom but the spitting crackle of the great fire, the after-echo of Feluce's voice, and the patter of the girl's feet.

The inn-keeper came through from the kitchen, bringing the stoups of ale himself. His face was as blank as ever as he set them down on a table by the hearth.

"Now," Feluce said, "we'll want some grilled fish, meat and vegetables, your most palatable cheese, fresh fruit, white bread and red wine."

"I'm afraid you'll be disappointed, sir," said the inn-keeper, very politely. "There's neither fish nor fruit to be had. I can let you have mutton and a few leeks, some ewe's milk cheese and a cup or two of berry liquor, which is all the wine we brew hereabouts. You must take us as you find us."

Feluce spat into the fire. His eyes shone cool and dangerous.

"Perhaps we should take our custom elsewhere."

"Perhaps you should."

The inn-keeper was a big man. Abruptly, he looked bigger. Feluce's hand whipped again to his sword. Havor stepped forward and struck the hand away.

"I beg your pardon, landlord. My companion was joking. We'll be happy to have whatever you can offer us."

The inn-keeper stared hard at Havor, who returned his scrutiny with a level emotionless look. The man nodded.

"Very good, sir." He turned and went out.

"Damn you, Havor," Feluce hissed. "Why didn't you let me deal with the oaf in my own way?"

"Your own way would have meant unnecessary trouble and no food."

Feluce swore and tossed off his ale, and soon the candle girl came back and laid their table, and a faint hum of talk started up in the room.

When the food arrived it was hot and good, despite the wrangling that had gone before.

Havor felt the fire and the supper and the thick tangy liquor exerting drowsy pressure on his awareness. But Kachil, who had only picked at his plate yet drunk freely from his goblet, was now glowing with wine and crackling with fever, giving bursts of wild stupid laughter, a perfect foil for Feluce's slightly slurred yet malicious wit.

Havor cursed them both, and the surge of despairing greed for Lukon's family that had partnered him with them. If he went above to sleep, God knew what they would be at. And even if he stayed down here, and strained open his eyes that watered for rest, and held his muscles taut and ready that were mewling at him to stretch out and dissolve, could he really hope to prevent the upheaval that now seemed somehow inevitable?

Feluce was banging on the table with his empty goblet, yelling for the inn-keeper.

The man came; it was his business to come when called. Yet he had a special look to him by now that intensified each time Feluce called him again.

"I've a generous mood on me tonight," Feluce told

him in a carrying voice. "Stoups of your finest ale all round."

The slight conversation in the room tailed off. In the past hour several had slipped out; by this time only nine or so men remained.

Shortly the ale came in and went round. Men stared down at it. Feluce raised his goblet and looked about expectantly. Nervously, men raised their own cups.

"Now," Feluce said, "since I am paying for it, I'll propose the toast. Which is—*the King!*"

Feluce drank, and affected surprise to see no one else drinking. "Come, *gentlemen,* this amounts to treason."

One by one the cups went up and the men drank.

Feluce laughed, pleased at the joke, while Kachil giggled and nodded insanely by the fire.

Feluce crashed down his goblet. "Where's the yellow-haired girl gone?"

The inn-keeper squared his shoulders. "Seeing to the pans," he said.

Feluce clicked his tongue against his teeth. "A great pity. That will turn her hands red and raw. Is she like your Lord's daughter in Avillis? I heard the witch also had yellow hair."

Kachil crowed with idiot mirth, but otherwise a peculiar addition of stillness had laid hold on the hall.

"No," the inn-keeper said in a strange voice, "she's my daughter, and the Lady of Avillis was above her in all things."

The words struck on Havor's ears oddly. The phrase sounded ritualistic, meant to appease, to ward off evil or anger—almost, a prayer, or as a man might touch wood.

"Well, well. Can your daughter sing, or dance? In the South we like to have entertainment with our supper."

"My daughter isn't a dancing girl, sir. As to singing, she's dumb from birth."

An urgent curious chill crept up Havor's spine. "No more, Feluce," he said.

"No more what, Havor? Nothing's happened yet. But I intend to liven up this dreary hole. Come on, landlord, bring your daughter out. Perhaps she can juggle the table knives if she won't dance or sing."

"My daughter has her work. In the kitchen."

"Oh? Stubborn, are you?" Feluce drained the last of his ale, then rose, strode up to the inn-keeper and lightly, smilingly, elbowed him aside.

Havor watched Feluce's slightly swaying figure pass through the lower door. In the thick silence of the room the crash of a pot came very clear, bright as a shower of sparks in the fire. Kachil's lunatic giggling started up again.

The inn-keeper's face was choked with color, a terrific rage held back. He too, it seemed, had heard the stories of the Bear King's vengeance on those who ill-used his soldiery.

Feluce re-emerged, pulling the blonde girl by her wrist. He dragged her to the space before the hearth where the table stood, and swung her up on it. He clapped his hands, stamped his feet, whistled a tune.

"Dance, girl. Quick! Round and round!"

The girl, plainly frightened nearly silly, began to circle wildly on the table.

Havor got to his feet, but at the same instant the inn-keeper moved, swift for his size, and Havor saw the leash of his rage had abruptly snapped. Before Feluce could dart aside or draw sword from scabbard, the man's fist had caught him a hammering blow that landed square on the chest. Feluce went reeling back, gasping, grabbed at the table but lost it, and fell against the long bench by the hearth. Havor saw the leather sack tip, tilt, and slide from the bench. It hit the stone-flag floor with the hollow ringing of a bell. Out rolled the harmless items with which they had packed it. The leather seemed to fold back in an uncanny and impossible way. Flame-light ran, suddenly piercing, on the golden rim of the Chalice.

There had been a silence before, a silence turgid and brooding. Now there came a new silence that made the silence before it sound like a crowd on market day. It seemed to well out of the very walls, up from the flags: a silence made of ancient fear and the generations who had known it. There was no movement either. Not a man stirred. Every eye was riveted to that one spot on the floor where the fire described, as if with frozen light, the round glittering mouth, and the black depth within it. Havor found himself considering, in a dreamlike troubled fashion, that he had never until now seen the great Chalice at this curious angle, and how, looking down into it, its vast beauty was lost, and it seemed more like a circular maw, wide open, waiting.

Then the inn-keeper was speaking, in a toneless soft voice that seemed loud in the room.

"I'd have put my ill-wish on you, men of the South. Now, you have my pity."

Feluce got up, with slitted gleaming eyes. He drew his sword, and poked at the inn-keeper's chest with the tip of it.

"I should kill you for daring to strike me."

The inn-keeper did not even look at him, only at the acid yellow brightness shining there on the floor. Feluce jabbed harder with the sword.

"Keep your eyes and your hands off that! The three of us have a certain interest in it. We're trained fighters, and we sleep light." He swung round. "And the rest of you will do well to remember what I say."

The empty pale faces stared back at him. The inn-keeper said, softly as before, "No man in Axa would touch that thing. Not if his wife and children were starving. Not to buy off the hangman's rope."

Feluce sheathed the sword, frowning. "I hope for the sake of your own miserable hide you're speaking the truth."

The girl had slid down from the table, her blonde hair hanging round her white face. She clung to her father's arm, and he half-turned to lead her away.

"Wait," Havor said.

The man halted but did not look back.

"So you know what we carry with us?"

"Yes, well enough. The Cup from Avillis."

"Why do you say you pity us?"

Still without turning, the inn-keeper said, "You will have time to discover."

He led the girl away into the kitchen, and the light there reddened and dimmed.

Outside, the winter winds were stirring, groping around the house. The street door banged. Havor glanced about, and saw that the room was now empty of everyone but themselves. He crossed to one of the big window places and looked out. Beyond the cloudy cockled glass, the narrow streets and leaning houses pressed back against a sky of racing, eagle-wing clouds. There seemed to be no lights in Axa.

A man screamed behind him. It was the kind of scream he had heard in battle—a cry of pain and terror and despair, a death-note. He spun about, his hand already on the knife.

Kachil was kneeling by the hearth, whimpering, his eyes fixed on the Chalice.

Havor went to him, and saw the sweat was standing out on the foxy face in great crystals.

"We must get him to bed," Havor said. "He's going crazy with fever."

Feluce shrugged.

The candles bobbed and smoked.

The boy who had stabled their horses crept in to take them up to their beds. He would not look in their faces, and kept well away from them, as if they carried some disease he feared to catch by touch. Feluce and Havor were forced to support Kachil up the wooden stairway, Feluce cursing every laborious step of the way. Havor got the red man between the covers, while Feluce stood idly leaning at the door.

"What a splendid nursemaid you are, Havor."

Havor did not reply. He was well used to Feluce and the manner of Feluce. Kachil was quieter now, and he seemed drowsing.

"With such tender care," Feluce said, "he'll no doubt recover his wretched health."

"Yes. He'll sweat tonight, but he should be easier tomorrow."

As Havor moved outside and shut the door of Kachil's chamber, Feluce said, "Of course, we could ride on, whether he's fit or not. That would make it half shares each in the gold . . ."

"So it would," Havor said, "but I'm not reckoning on changing our plans. As you saw, I put the sack in my own room, and I, too, Feluce, sleep light."

Feluce caught something in Havor's eyes and voice. Lightly he murmured, "Oh, so the hawk has hawk's talons, too. Well, well. I commend your sense of honor."

In his own chamber Havor unbuckled the clinging cold mail, drew off his boots, and stretched out on the bed under the thick rugs. Yet he had kept on his shirt and breeches, and laid the sheathed knife ready under the pillow. Not Feluce alone, but also the dark inn, with its dark superstition, had made him wary.

He had been heavy with sleep before, yet now sleep hung back, like an obstinate, half-wild horse which follows you where you would rather it did not, and runs off when you call it with the bridle and bit in your hand. Still, he was comfortable enough. He could hear the wind as it gurned and buffeted the corners of the house, but here was a warm world, and it was good to lie soft—for, though the bed was a hard one, the ground outside Avillis had been harder. And before that, how often he had lain on other ground, rolled in his cloak on the stone floor by some dying inn fire, or, on the march, billeted on some unwilling house, in a loft or freezing barn. And now he had spent his money freely, as had the other two, on a dinner and a private chamber. Feluce and Kachil trusted the Chalice would cover all extravagance when they sold it at Venca. And he? Well, there would be other work, another trade, at the end of this journey, once he had taken his portion of gold to that lonely infertile farm, and the three waiting there for Lukon.

Poor Lukon, Havor suddenly thought. Whatever else I've lost or never had, I've life. And it's dear to me.

Kachil opened one eye, cautiously.

He could not remember where he was, and an immediate feeling of miserable apprehension came over him. He had so often woken up like this and found himself in jail, or the cellar of some petty nobleman's house. He knew what was in store. He would be systematically starved, lashed and clouted until they had got all his stolen spoils from him—whether hidden about his person or in the byways outside—then they would throw him back in the street. Kachil's life had always run in a circle of thieving, violence and destitution, followed inevitably by further thieving; he could see no way to get free of it.

He had a kind of cunning, but no real cleverness, and above all, no luck.

However, this was not a prison. It was an inn. Kachil opened the other eye, and stretched in the odd restricted manner of a man trying not to attract attention.

The taproom looked familiar, but he could not recall being here before. There were dingy windows, and a big fire that was making him hot. He noticed now that his precautions had been unnecessary; the whole boiling stuffy room was empty. Or was it?

In a far corner he gradually made out a slim cloaked form, and a girl's profile like a white cameo. Very slowly, the cameo turned and looked at Kachil, and directed him, by the slightest inclination of the head, to approach.

Kachil was surprised, wary, flattered, scared. He got up, glad enough to leave the fire because he was so unpleasantly warm, yet the heat seemed to pursue him across the room.

Again the lady gave a brief nod, though she did not speak. He sat down opposite, and saw what she had before her.

It was a box of the little painted two-faced bricks with which fortune-tellers played. You shook the box, turned out three or four, and the faces they showed were symbols of your fate. Such things bothered Kachil. Like most people dogged by ill-luck, he had acquired a respect for it. Besides, he could see at a glance that the way the bricks had fallen for the girl was bad. A skull was uppermost, a broken ring and a burning tower. Yet she smiled to herself, tipping the bricks into the box and offering it to him.

"Oh, no, lady," Kachil said. "I don't care to. I'd rather wait and see—"

But she smiled again, shook the box herself and cast out the bricks before him.

Kachil started, and sweat blurred his eyes. There was a skull for him, too, and the arrow that meant sickness, and a strangler's noose.

"That's a sour box-full you have there, lady," he said jokingly, dry-mouthed.

As if she agreed, the girl left the bricks lying and stood up. Kachil, bewildered, found he must go after her.

She opened the door into the street. The wind blew in. He had hoped the winter night would cool him, but it did not. There seemed to be flames in his belly and temples. He could get no relief.

The wind had thrust off the woman's hood, and spread out her hair like a saffron fan. Something about her hair disturbed Kachil a great deal.

Then he saw the dark carriage on the road, the dark horses with blond manes. Two shadowy figures waited, and the carriage door stood wide. Surely this was the lady's conveyance, yet the figures did not offer to help her inside—it was to Kachil they courteously beckoned with their long thin hands.

And abruptly he was in their grasp. They were lifting him, swinging him up, and he was silently struggling and fighting to no avail. One last glimpse he had of the lady's smile and her spreading hair before he fell into the carriage.

Why was it so airless, so lightless, so muffled? And why did the door now seem to open in the top, not in the side as with other vehicles? And the interior was extraordinarily narrow—

Suddenly he knew, and as he knew, the door slammed down over him, blotting out everything.

Kachil writhed and strained. He was shut in a coffin, shut in with heat and blind smother. He was stifling—and at that moment he felt something stir, soft against his neck and chin, a moving blanket coming to cover him. Kachil chittered with terror. It felt like—like hair . . . A strand settled gently, ticklingly, on his lips, then another. Now it was snowing hair in the dark. He thrashed out, he choked. He tried to fill his bursting lungs, and the blackness exploded in his chest and brain.

There seemed to Havor to be no margin between waking and sleeping. Suddenly his warm bed was gone, and he had forgotten it. He was riding on an empty road at midnight.

Only the wind had followed him into the dream, the cold, yearning, wolf-voiced wind.

There was no other sound.

A white light sailed high; he looked up at it, thinking to see the moon, but saw instead a pearly skull set in the sky, grinning, ribboning worms of clouds threading its eye-sockets.

He glanced back then. Behind him on the pale road was a funeral procession: black banners, a gilded hearse with a canopy of inky velvet, jet-black horses with ice-white manes, striking sparks from their stamping hooves.

Fear swelled over Havor, a fear to which he could put no name. He urged his own horse to flight, but it could not, or would not, move, only stamped with its feet like the others, while its own dun mane bleached slowly to the color of salt.

The wind screamed.

The screaming woke him. And he found it was not part of the dream but a man's voice somewhere in the house, wailing in horror.

"Kachil," he said aloud.

The memory of the dream clung round the room like a broken, floating web.

Havor left the bed and dragged up his cloak. The inn seemed dankly cold now. Kachil's fever must be worse to make him scream like that. Havor had seen such fevers before, and realized the man would need watching if he were to get through to morning. Havor did not relish the task, but he had come across a deal of pain and loneliness, and his own nature had imposed a certain duty on him towards others.

He struck flame and lit a candle stump. Huddled in the cloak, he pushed open his door and went out. Kachil had fallen quiet now, and the whole inn was thick with silence, as before.

It was black outside the door, a blackness the little flickering tallow seemed incapable of piercing. Kachil's chamber lay around a turn in the passage, just past the place where a crack of window opened in the wall. The grey glass was on fire with moonlight, yet, like the candle, seemed unable to cast its light beyond itself into the dark.

Havor was a yard or so away when a figure moved out of the shadow and up against the window pane—a girl's figure, slender, unmistakable, though all a flat black cutout on the moon-flare. He thought it must be the innkeeper's daughter, the fair-haired, frightened, dumb maid, roused, as he had been, by Kachil's cries. So he called out to her softly, "Don't be afraid. I'll see to him."

The silhouette seemed to flicker as shapes will when set against strong light. Then it slipped sideways and vanished back into the dark. When he passed the window, the shadows were empty. Even so, he thought he should come up with her when he turned the corner. When he did not, an odd creeping unease beset him. He put it aside like the wisps of the dream, and eased open Kachil's door.

The feeble light drew out a muddled form on the bed, a man's arm outflung on the pillow, and, as Havor set down the lump of wax on the stool, a long glinting paleness on his own sleeve. He picked it off. The flame slid stickily on its thinness. A single golden hair.

When he let go of it it spiralled down on to the rugs of the bed. Havor checked. He lifted up the candle again, examining the rugs closely. He was remembering the horse-dealer's dog, in the East, which had slept every night across his master's legs, and left in the morning, as a token of its presence, a sheen of coarse brindled hairs on the old rogue's trousers. Now it seemed a great dog had been sleeping across Kachil, an impossibly huge dog, covering him from crown to toe. A dog with hairs as fine and long and golden as those from the head of a fair young girl.

The candle flame fluttered, and passed over Kachil's face. His eyes and mouth were wide open, but his body was as cold and as lifeless as the night.

4. The Road

DAWN HAD WATERED THE DARKNESS to a sullen ivory, and the sun rose like a dim cheap jewel of glass.

There seemed no one stirring at the inn, and Feluce, despite his boast, appeared to have slept very deep, and still to be sleeping.

In the taproom the great fire had become a heap of ashes. Chill morning light washed through the wide windows, making the room seem larger, emptier, unnaturally colorless and grim.

"Landlord!" Havor called. To his own ears his voice sounded flat and uncarrying. But after a while the man came through into the big room, and his face was blank as paper, as before.

"What can I do for you, sir?"

Havor said, "One of my companions died in the night."

Curiously, he had expected no surprise or any other emotion from the inn-keeper, no distress or half-hidden sour gladness. And indeed, the man folded his arms and stared back at Havor as if he had merely spoken of the day or the state of the road.

"Do you have a priest in Axa?"

"Yes."

Havor waited some moments for him to go on, then asked, "Where can I find him?"

"You won't. Not unless you go the twenty miles to Osil. He's there at present on church business, and not due back till next holy day. You'll get no priest-burial in Axa."

"Then we must make our own, and beg spades."

The inn-keeper said quietly, "You'll get neither spade to dig nor earth to put him in, here."

"Let's be clear," Havor said. "The soldier I refer to wasn't the one who caused you trouble at supper. It was the red-haired man, who had the fever. He died of it."

"You think so?"

The dry wind beating at the house seemed to catch Havor coldly between the shoulder blades.

"Yes, landlord, I think so. What is it you think?"

"I think Axa will be glad to see you gone, you and your friends, quick or dead."

"Your daughter," Havor said. "What was she after in the passage in the dark? A look at what we carry?"

"My daughter? She never stirred out."

"Some other maid of the house, then. I saw a girl by the window, near the sick man's room, last night."

For the first time the inn-keeper's face betrayed itself. He smiled, a twisted stone-eyed smile. "Very likely," he said.

Havor looked at him and said no more.

He went instead to rouse Feluce, and then out into the town to buy a spade with which to dig Kachil a resting place.

The sky was now a blowing mass of white curded

cloud, and the wind had teeth in it. The crow in the brass cage by the inn door was huddled into a ragged clot of feathers. On the streets nothing moved.

Havor walked for some while. Sometimes he glimpsed a face peering from an upper window, hastily vanishing as he glanced up at it. Once he came upon a solitary child playing a game with smooth pebbles in an alley, but it sprang up and darted away when it saw him. News, it seemed, went fast in Axa, and now he was shunned. He had seen lepers treated so, or the sick in time of plague. His skin crept and the wind gnawed on him.

Eventually he heard start up the dull yet piercing strokes of a smith's hammer. Turning down a narrow street he came on a blacksmith's. It was open at front, all scarlet gloom within, and pulsing shadow. Gradually Havor made out the big dark shape of a man who flung down ringing blows on the anvil in a repeating clock-work motion and with a sound that tore at ears and belly in the still, brittle air.

Havor stood at the wide doormouth, and after a while the man left off beating, sensing him there, sensing he would not go away. Without turning, the smith straightened, and the forge flame ran in limpid, russet streams along the outline of his bare arms, knotted and glowing like metal too, while the quiet dinned with the memory of hammer strokes.

"What is it you're wanting?"

"The town appears uncommonly empty," Havor said. The smith kept his back to him and did not answer. "Why not keep indoors with the rest?"

"Keeping indoors brings no work and no wage."

"I want something," Havor said, "with which to dig a man's grave."

"A friend's grave?"

"A man I travelled with on the road."

"You'll not be grieving then. Why bother with a burial? The wolves'd thank you."

"Will you sell me a spade?" Havor said softly.

"In the corner," the smith said.

He did not look behind him as Havor crossed the forge and took up the iron-bladed tool.

"How do you value it?"

"I'll take no payment," the smith said.

"It seems I must dig outside Axa. You won't get it back."

"I'd not take it back," the smith said, "once it had been in your hands."

Havor walked about the anvil, stood facing the smith across it, and found a granite, wincing control on the large metallic-sweating face.

"A Chalice," Havor said very clearly, "made of gold."

The smith picked up his hammer once again and brought it down between them, murderously. Violet sparks flew, sizzling. But his eyes had a blind look. He might have been alone.

Havor took the spade and walked back to the inn, through the deserted streets.

"What fools," Feluce crowed. "What *fools!*"

They were riding, still following the road, Axa now only a smudge of ruddy walls on the distance behind them.

Kachil lay across his mount, wrapped in a blanket. Havor had tied the horse by a rope to his own saddle. Feluce, going a little ahead, the wind licking and smoothing his pale bright hair like an invisible cat's tongue, laughed again.

The inn-keeper had refused their money. The supper, the fine private chambers and warm beds had all been gratis. They had carried the Dark Lord's Chalice out of

Avillis. Now not a man in Axa would take coin from them, or shelter them another night, or let them put Kachil under the earth inside the walls.

About three or four miles from Axa there began to be open stretches between the trees. Soon Havor dismounted, tethered his horse and started to dig.

Feluce sat watching him. Presently he said, "I hope you understand, Havor, I'm not thinking of turning grave-digger. You can do all that yourself since it bothers you." Havor said nothing. The spade bit into the dark moist soil. "Better make it good and deep. You won't want the wolves to spoil your handiwork."

After a time, Feluce began to gnaw on a nail and fell silent, and only the spade made sound.

Havor thought nothing as he dug out the pit. Sometimes the blade struck rock, then he would shift a little. When it was ready, he lifted Kachil down, and set him in the shadowy crumbling oval, and climbed out. And then an abrupt picture came into his mind of tree growths and rank flowers springing from this earth, nourished by Kachil beneath, and, with that, a bursting wave of pity and regret. For though he had scarcely known Kachil, the fox-faced thief, Havor seemed to see the meanness and poverty of his life, all the chances missed and now lost for ever. And out of Havor's mouth, as if of themselves, came the few disjointed words of a half-recollected prayer.

Feluce jeered at him.

"The unbeliever chanting over the damned!"

They went on, after, leaving Kachil quiet under his new earth blanket, Havor still leading the third horse that no one would buy in Axa. He left the spade, leaning, in the trees.

The daylight flickered around them, hardened. Overhead the blowing clouds moved more slowly, filmed with a smoky daffodil light. The road, as Havor had imagined before, seemed to reflect perfectly the colors of the sky, as if it were made of solid water, or smooth unglittering glass.

At noon they ate pieces of black bread, and drank the flat ale—soldiers' journey-food, that they took as they rode. They came by a village but it was deserted and desolate. Venca was still days off—Venca, with its wide streets, and merchants' houses and jewellers' shops.

"Do you still have it?" Feluce said abruptly.

"You know."

"Let me see it, then. Come on. Let me look at the gold."

Havor lifted up the sack, opened it, let Feluce gaze down past the golden rim and the eyes of gems into that void of darkness held between.

Feluce reached with a finger, and delicately stroked the Chalice. "Only two, now," he said. "Half-shares after all." He looked up. Charmingly he said, "Did you kill Kachil, Havor? You were so against abandoning him, and yet he died, and you found him. Or was it the other way about?"

There came a change in the cloud above, a sudden heaviness, a shadow.

"There's snow coming," Havor said. "We'd better get on."

Feluce smiled. After a moment or so, he said, "I wonder what she looked like, Havor, the Lady of Avillis. The Magus' daughter. Goldenhead."

"You'll never know."

"But I do know—in a fashion. I dreamed about her, last night. Long blowing tassels of saffron hair and a black gown with blue dazzles on it. Holding the Chalice in her white hands." He grinned. "If I believed in such stuff, I'd get some spirit-raiser to call her up, just so I could get a look at her, awake."

There was tinsel on the air. Pale motes began to touch their skin, melt on the manes of the horses.

Havor glanced back, over his shoulder. He had not looked there before, not since he put Kachil in the earth. Through the white, bee-swarming snow, he saw . . . something. Something moving, something that seemed to alter shape, become another thing.

"Oh, yes. Our fellow travellers are still there," Feluce remarked jauntily. "Odd they never came to Axa while we were in it. If we stopped, waited, perhaps they'd come up with us."

"We agreed we don't want company," Havor said.

Feluce only grinned into the snow. Havor noticed a thread, coiled like a snake on Feluce's sleeve, and another on his collar—two gold silks that did not match his own white blondness.

Half a mile farther on they came to a ruined tower, a broken shadow bulking through the snow like a dark-mantled ghost, for some climbing plant had crawled all over it. It was a watch-post of an earlier time—an earlier king, perhaps, who had made war and had left his garrison here afterwards.

It offered no shelter; they would have ridden by, but something crept out, and stood on the road.

It was difficult to see anything clearly. Startled, Feluce's horse flung up its forefeet, pawing the snow, Feluce righted it with a cuff and an oath. Havor made out a woman's shape in front of them, a woman muffled like the tower, in a dark mantle. His heart sent a sudden gonging panic through his body. But it was only a peasant-woman, old, bent over, he now saw, with wild crazy eyes set in creases of snake-skin.

Feluce gave a shout at her.

"Out of the path, old crone!"

But she did not stir.

"What do you want?" Havor asked, leaning to her a little way. Perhaps she was a beggar, starving in the cold. . . . His hand went towards the money in his shirt, and at once she called, thin as the cry of some animal or bird in the stark woods:

"Give me nothing of yours!"

"What then?" he said.

"Hawk," she said. "Hawk and cat. Fox gone. Fox dead. Fox, then cat, then hawk."

Feluce smiled. "What a sweet old babbler. You should watch your tongue."

Havor thought: How does she know about Kachil, the fox? I buried him miles back. She can't have seen and then come on so far, on her own, in the cold.

"I understand things," she said, as if she read his thoughts. "Bird-flight, leaf-fall, cloud-shape. They have their meanings."

"Can you call up the dead?" Feluce asked her. His eyes sparkled, there was colour in his cheeks as if he were excited or pleased.

The old woman looked at him, her head held slightly sideways. She, too, grinned, but her teeth were decayed. She seemed now like a bird of prey.

"No need," she croaked, "no need. Only be patient."

"Is there a town soon on the road?" Havor asked sharply.

When she stopped looking at Feluce, and looked instead at him, she seemed to alter, change, become more ordinary, again nothing but a wasted peasant-woman.

"Arnos. You'll not come to it before dark, if then."

Feluce reached down to her, touched her shoulder.

"How about giving us shelter in your own place, old lady?"

"Too far, and far too small to house you. But you'll find a lodging on the road tonight. And perhaps, a meeting."

And again they were both grinning, drawn close in their weird swift conspiracy, the young, smooth-fleshed man, handsome, easy, only the cruel mouth to betray his malice and the spike of tongue behind the strong white teeth, and the old skull-faced beldame, with her dragon-scale eyes and dirty fangs, and the note of promise in her voice. Havor felt the hair shift on his neck; his spine crawled with silver ants. He shook himself free of them, picked out a coin from the bag about his neck, and threw it at the crone.

She jumped back with a thin hoarse squeak as if he had slung a burning coal at her instead of a copper bit.

The coin lay on the paving. She jerked her head like a viper, and spat between herself and it. Then she slipped back, by the tower, into the wood, behind the curtain of the snow.

Feluce began to sing. His voice came melodious and certain. He spurred his horse and rode fast, setting the pace up the blurred stretch of the road.

The snow filled Havor's eyes; he blinked it away. He had once seen a bridegroom go like that to his marriage—a young joyful boy hurrying to wed a girl he had wanted and worked to get for half a year.

And perhaps, a meeting.

At Havor's stirrup the Chalice rang like a bell. The rhythm of the bell bemused him.

The night began to change the colors of the world. Lavender gloaming, and snow like the falling feathers of a pale blue bird. They were still galloping, Feluce in the lead. Havor seemed to see Feluce very clearly and very minutely, and in great detail: a tiny toy figure, a mailed soldier doll with hair dyed violet by the dusk, riding a wooden puppet horse with racing legs, its body sleek as metal, its eyes and nostrils wet magenta stars burning through the swirling flakes of twilight.

Then, out of the vague blueness, a darker, more solid blueness. Nothing seemed real. The new image less real than all the rest. Had they reached Arnos after all, and was it a phantom town, called up by the old witch, a place built of smoke, surrounded by walls of cloud?

As they came closer, Havor made out size and shape. No town, but a mansion: towers and a ruinous gate, a deserted pile, stranded at the roadside.

The snow stopped as they rode nearer.

At some time there had been a fire inside the mansion. It had been scoured out by fire like oyster from within shell, or marrow from within bone gouged by the teeth of a starving dog. It was entirely, mercilessly gutted. Only a mask remained.

5. Night

THE LAND AND THE SKY turned black with night, but the land glinted with the pale stencilling of snow over its darkness.

Beyond the circle of their fire, rose the crochet-work of the ruin, which had seen other, more far-ranging flames. Beyond that lay the strange and silent landscape, the grey-white slash of the road with nothing moving on it, and no sound save the low snow-wind breathing over the emptiness.

They had fed their horses and eaten, such as their own meal was. In the incredible quiet, Feluce, in his excited impatience, seemed to glow, to kindle and flare like the fire, or like a man with a fever; like Kachil. He cracked jokes, spoke of his family in the South—the fat cloth-vendor, the over-fond mother, or else of the sly adventures of his time with the army. His talk came fast and fluid. Havor listened, but scarcely spoke a word. He watched Feluce. He had never seen or heard Feluce before in such a mood, and all the time a pressing, tomb-cold dread worked in the dim background of Havor's thoughts. He was afraid, or rather, he knew that soon he would be afraid. Fear, like an expected guest, was waiting at the mind's door.

Once he fancied he heard a wolf's long-drawn howling. He strained his ears but heard no more of it. It was odd; they should have called more often, for the woods must be alive with the wolf-kind, now the first snows were down.

Feluce lay on his elbow, looking at the leather sack with the Chalice in it, smiling, as if he and it shared a secret between them. Presently he rolled himself in his blanket and seemed ready for sleep.

"A moonless night," Havor said. "Perhaps we should set a watch. I'll take the first. I'll wake you—"

"No you won't, by heaven. I'm for bed, such as it is. And sweet dreams." Feluce chuckled.

As Havor watched him, he smilingly shut his eyes and seemed to sleep at once. The fire cast bronze-red colour on his face. After a moment he turned on his side, away from Havor's gaze.

The wind whistled far off, or close, through the gaping lattices of the old mansion.

Havor fed sticks to the blaze, but a somber weariness crept over him. He glanced about. The night was empty. He lay down as Feluce had done.

He thought: I have nothing to fear.

Nothing to fear as yet, he thought.

Suddenly there was a great moon overhead. A huge, round, corn-yellow moon, carved out of amber or beaten from gold, the size of a water-wheel on the sky. And against the yellow round, Havor made out three smokes that formed and solidified and became three silhouettes. Two tall men with hard clean lines about them, one hooded, one with a helm of sorts on his head, a helm with two twisted horns that interlocked with each other at the tips. Between the two men was a girl with long hair blowing ink-black across the vivid topaz. They were Giants in the air.

So this was where fear was waiting, here, in sleep, as he had guessed.

Havor struggled to wake, but already the shapes on the moon were fading, the moon itself going out like a guttering lamp. This night was not for him. A deeper, darker region of sleep pulled him down. He sank like lead in the billows, and fear, and all other things, were drowned there with him.

Feluce woke at the mansion gate. He woke expectantly and was not disappointed. There was a great change in everything.

The mansion was whole, and full of light as if it burned again within. On the gate-pillars two torches flared inside tubes of colored glass, sparking green and ruby stains on the open iron gates and the broad chip-stone ride beyond. Feluce crossed the ride and mounted the steps.

Here, big carved-wood doors stood open too—wide open on the glow within—and stone birds of prey, with eyes of polished quartz, creakily swivelled their necks to stare at him as he went between them. He laughed at them, pleased at their antics, uncaring whether they were mechanical or enchanted.

The floors of the mansion were laid with small chequers, black and scarlet and white; he came through another pair of open doors, this time inlaid with gold, and found a banqueting hall.

Some of the lamps here were of blue and amethyst and blood-red glass, so that the place pulsed with extraordinary colors. Draperies and tapestries hung down the walls, each worth a fortune that Feluce, son of a cloth-vendor in the South, could not help but value with a sly and sideways look. The long table was lit by tall candles in gold sconces, piled with steaming roasts and fragrant cakes and fruits and crystal flagons of wine, as if everything had just been brought in from the kitchens and set down. Somewhere music was playing, very soft, but no musicians showed themselves.

There were four gold chairs set at the table. At head and foot sat two black-cloaked men—his hosts. Facing Feluce across the board was the lady he had waited all this while to see. As soon as he looked at her, she rose and came around the table towards him, and she was everything he had expected, and more.

Her skin was pale and smooth as vellum, her hair not blowing wild now but intricately dressed in loops and curls, with strings of round white pearls wound through. Her brows and her long thick lashes were gold as the gilt fringe on the robe of a priest, though her eyes were black and shining like the eyes of the stone birds at the door. She wore a gown of dark blue velvet, the shade of a midsummer midnight, and a girdle of gold serpents twisted about each other with sapphires dripping from their mouths.

She smiled at Feluce, and, putting her hand lightly through his arm, led him to the table. He was to sit facing her, between the two dark men. Both were masked in black velvet, both wore gauntlets of black leather stitched with gold; he scarcely glanced at them, he was so taken with his lady. His fond mother had always said, had she not, that her fine handsome son would make a good marriage, far above his station?

The man on Feluce's left poured him wine, the other carved him meat. Feluce ate and drank hungrily. Never had he tasted such food or liquor. His hosts did not touch a morsel to their lips, but it did not seem strange to him. Neither did they speak to him, or to each other, but this also did not trouble him at all.

Yet he was careful not to stuff himself. He sensed the courteous and formal, and presently his shrewdness was proved lucky, for the fair lady rose and offered him her hand, and he somehow understood that they would dance together.

It was a stately dance, a dance of the Northern cities that he did not know, yet by some means he was able to execute the steps elegantly, as if he did, for which he was thankful. When it was finished, his partner led him away from the table and through a curtained arch into another smaller room, where the lamps were green and indigo, and a sunken pool lay in the middle of the floor.

It was a very pretty room, a useless plaything of a room for the rich.

Out of the single nostril of a strange stone beast a fountain shot in a diamond arc, splintering the smooth water at its center. The pool was green, and full of the darting of bright jewelled fish.

At the edge of the water the Lady of Avillis halted, and gave him her fingers to kiss.

Until that moment, Feluce had been excited and full of himself and his success. But as his lips touched the cool pale texture of her hand, a coldness seemed to seep up through them from her skin, and down, into his body.

And then both her white hands slipped by his face, and fastened about his throat.

A wind burst through the room, blowing in the tall windows as it came, with a sound of broken ice. It was a black wind too, it extinguished the colored lamps, and in the fluttering darkness Feluce found that it was no longer the girl who embraced his neck, but a tall, dark shadow, with a pair of hands sharp, cruel and unbending as claws or talons. Feluce clutched at them and felt, not a gauntlet under his frenzied fingers, nor even flesh, but hard, nerveless ridges of bone. The hands of a skeleton strangled him.

Feluce gave a choked scream. He beat against the shadowy figure, which gave off a dull and terrible rattling through its garments, while in the eye-holes of the mask were two black gapes of nothing.

Struggling, Feluce slipped sideways and fell, and then came the burning cold shock of the pool about his body, the water at his ribs, the floor slippery under his feet. But the shadow had not let go of him; it had leaped down too. And now, with a strength beyond any Feluce had ever encountered, it thrust him backwards into a freezing liquid fire, and an emerald darkness stopped his mouth and sight.

Havor opened his eyes to a dawn sky netted with cobweb clouds, the sun a decaying rose behind them.

He was very cold, very cramped. He had slept deeply, and the heaviness of that sleep was still on him. The fire was out.

He rose stiffly, stretching, not aware yet of anything wrong, or any expectancy that it should be so. Then, as he bent to kindle a flame again among the wood, he noticed that Feluce was gone.

He turned at once to look at the Chalice, and saw it filling the sack, as before. He saw Feluce's blanket on the ground where he had rolled himself in it. The three horses waited, shivering, where they had been tethered.

Havor trudged across the broken paving to one of the many huge rents in the mansion's sides, and stared out. Unbroken snow, packed hard, black bone woods. No smoke, no noise, no speck of life.

Havor came back and stood by the grey dead fire. After a time, he called, "Feluce!"

Somewhere old timber cracked in the cold. Nothing else answered him.

Havor crossed the gaping, characterless expanse, picking between the holes and the jagged debris where the roof had come down. He went through a place where there had been double doors, and, beyond, the floor was thick and winking with a tiny crushed glitter of colored glass.

It had been a banqueting hall, he saw; he noted the long, metal table, twisted from the heat of the fire. A huge beam had fallen across it.

There was an arch in the wall, and after that a piece of a room, opened above and on two sides to the biting winter day. In the middle of the floor lay a stagnant shallow pool, the water scaled over above with a crackling greenish ice, though near the pool's lip the ice had been broken and scattered.

Havor went close, and looked down.

He looked through murk and shadows and ice and stray reflections of the sky, straight into a pair of wide-open eyes.

A deadly sick realization gripped Havor, like a fog in his throat and brain.

Feluce lay under the pool, which had been just deep enough to drown him. And, as Havor gazed down into that fixed, returning gaze, something stirred a little, coming to the surface. A handful of hair, a long, golden, shining eddy, turning now on a small wind-created current.

I am next, then, Havor thought. And fear, the expected guest, came through the open door, into his mind.

He went to the horses and mounted the black, leading the other two as he had led Kachil's yesterday. The wind blew claws, but he scarcely felt them. The Chalice jolted at his knee, hanging from the saddle.

Half a mile from the ruin he looked back, over his shoulder, along the way. There was something there, a shadow-shape, a reflection, a cloud.

Alone, he still had company on the road. Would have it till he died.

6. Afternoon in Arnos

AFTERNOON LIMPED INTO ARNOS, sour and yellow under the low sky.

The streets were empty, snow lying along the alleys, up against the narrow doors. Only a hunch-backed dwarf, crouching for pennies in the gate-porch, heard hooves, and looked up to see the soldier ride past on his black horse, leading two others by a rope.

The dwarf ran out and held up his begging cup.

The soldier turned in his saddle, produced a coin; then seemed to hesitate a moment, recollecting something. But the dwarf's eager, desperate face appeared to decide him. He dropped the bright coin into the cup.

"Tell me, where's the priest's house, hereabouts?"

The dwarf shook his head, pointed to his lips. He was dumb.

"Can you show me then?"

The dwarf grinned and scampered up the street, glancing back from time to time, like a dog, to see if the soldier were following.

In this fashion they moved along the alleys and thoroughfares of Arnos, the dwarf skittering ahead, the soldier riding slowly after, and came to a square where a crumbling church leant up against the neighboring walls of small houses. At the right hand of these the dwarf pointed. The house of the priest.

Havor stared at the house, the leaning church. His eyes smarted from the cold. The poverty of these buildings dejected him. There could be little hope in them. But then, could he really say he had come here to be given hope, or courage, or some sort of shield? He had actually expected nothing. It occurred to him that he was completing a ritual of some kind, an actor playing a part, a show that must be got perfect and gone through without a word lost or a gesture left out, but which meant nothing to him as a man, which had no place or function in his darkening world.

He caught himself noting every detail of the church. It was very old, its tower rising in three tiers of brown stone, with narrow black window slots. Light painted its one sunward side; shadows nudged the other. The "O" of the holy circle at its summit was inscribed in silver on the ochre clouds.

He had seen men going to their deaths. Some went proud and blind, some lost in panic, crying out. Others went like this, staring at objects on the way—a pebble, a blade of grass—as if trying to memorize them, carry their shape, hue, texture, every grain and mote, beyond the cord or the axe-man's stroke.

Havor wrenched his attention from the tower, and looked back for the dwarf. But the little man had run off, the bright coin in his bowl that might carry a leper's taint on it now.

There was a rail before the church. Havor tethered the three horses there. He untied the leather sack, and left it lying in the shadowy house porch.

He went into the deep mouth of the church, drawn abruptly by some childhood recollection.

Dim, dusty, bare. The long aisle, the echoing floor between slender columns like ghost's fingers, the banners, ancient muddied crimson and tarnished gold, drooping their wings above the altar, the watch-light in its green glass, the sallow tapers lit in flame-beaded ranks.

He stood before the carved circle, and remembered how the priests had beaten him when he was five years old because he had said the thing reminded him of a cartwheel.

A hand fell suddenly on his shoulder. It was like a hand reaching out of his childhood. He felt the stinging raw teeth of the thongs across his back, and spun about, his own hand on the knife hilt.

The priest was about thirty, stern and strong and tall, a man who looked as if he could handle a blade too, or a stave, if he had need for it. His glance had noted Havor's weapon belt, but he said, "I didn't intend to startle you, soldier, but you wear Southern mail, and God knows, what little we have worth stealing, we value."

A brave man, Havor thought. He knew the ways of the South, and stood unarmed to talk of them.

"I'm not here to steal from you, father," Havor said. "I'm here to ask you questions."

The priest smiled. "Part of my work is to find answers to questions, soldier. Upon what matter?"

"Avillis. And the dead Lord of Avillis."

The priest left off smiling. The corners of his eyes tightened. He said, "I trust you've good reason to ask me. I trust there's much at stake."

"My life," Havor said.

Until that moment there had been a kind of denial in him still. Speaking these words banished it. He saw the vast black pit rise up from the yellow rim and yawn for him, and the priest, looking in his face, seemed to see it too.

"Come with me," he said, and, saluting the altar, he turned and led Havor out of the church, and into his house. At the porch Havor again picked up the leather sack; the priest said nothing.

It was mean enough, the house, bare as the church without the church's rotted splendor. It was dark, too; the priest took down a little lamp from a shelf and lighted it. No fire burned on the hearth despite the bitter cold.

The priest sat and motioned Havor to do likewise. Then a silence fell, which somehow fed upon itself, swelling until it seemed that neither of them could ever break it.

Finally Havor spoke.

"I've no doubt you've had news of Avillis, somehow, the way news seems to get around ahead of itself in the country."

"Yes. There was news in the northern sky, too, some three days back—red light and red smoke."

"Avillis burning," Havor said. "The Southern King took her, the Black Bear of the South. His armies sacked her after."

"So much I might guess," the priest said.

"Then can you guess what this might be?"

The priest shrank back and his face whitened, slowly, to the colour of bleached wood. "I've heard of such a thing—a great Cup of gold—"

Havor let the leather fall down on to the floor, and held the Chalice on his knee. The whole room seemed to burn with it; it seemed to shine through his hands as though they were transparent, as a lamp flame shows up the red blood in the fingers.

"Two men and I took this thing from the rubble of the Lord's palace in Avillis. One man died of a fever, the other drowned. Something came after us from the city. I imagine it will have me, next."

The priest said hoarsely, "You're superstitious, then? You believe in the undead?"

"No father, I believe my eyes. Three riders trailed us on the road, one with a yellow hood, which I saw today was really her yellow hair, for they've followed me close since sun-up."

The priest's eyes had fixed on Havor's hands. Havor looked down, and found that he had begun to caress the Chalice, as if it were some favorite animal, or the hair of a girl he loved.

"As you see," he said, and stilled the action. "What now? Is my death certain?"

"I don't know," the priest said in a low, sick voice. "I don't know. But I tell you this. You must not sleep a single night until you've rid yourself of that."

"Then tell me where to be rid of it, father. Here, in the church?"

"No! By heaven, not here—nowhere on the old road. Pagans and men of a dark age built it. It would direct evil, and the power of evil, as tall trees direct lightning. Can you get to Venca? The road ends there, in the fields, half a mile out. And there's the great church there, with the relics of saints. . . . Perhaps there's help for you in that place."

"Perhaps and perhaps," Havor said. "And it's three days still to Venca, isn't it? What if I simply leave the Chalice in Arnos, in some gutter, or outside some shut door?"

The priest's pale face grew stern. "Then you bring on the innocent the curse your greed brought on yourself. Any place you leave it, it will poison. Besides which, they have your scent, the pack that follows you. It would need strong words, strong wills, to save you. At Venca, perhaps—"

"And perhaps not," Havor said, and at the center of his being a huge clock seemed to strike, and then fall silent.

"Just so," said the priest, and lowered his steady gaze.

Havor drew up the leather sack. The glory of the gold sank down and emptied the room of its fire.

"You fool!" the priest suddenly cried out angrily. "Had you never heard a single tale of them, those three, the Lord and his son and his daughter? That Cup there, brimmed with blood, used to honor the most black, the most foul—" He broke off. As Havor reached the door, he said, more softly, "Do you have the holy circle on your sword, man?"

"Yes," Havor said, "but it will be no use to me because I have no faith in it. Good-day, father, and thanks for your advice."

The priest bowed his head, and presently he heard the sound of hooves in the street outside, but the feel of death stayed for a long while at his elbow, in the little room.

The red round sun was very low now. Havor saw it sometimes between the roofs as he rode the winding hill-streets of Arnos.

The leather sack, when he had tied it again on his saddle, seemed heavier, as if the Chalice had grown more weighty. As if two men's deaths had filled the black pit under its rim, or possibly his own death, which was to come.

How would it be?

The key to Kachil had been superstition and fear, to Feluce—ambition and pleasure. And to himself, the key was—what?

I could ride out of town, he thought, sit down by the road and wait for night, and for them. Easy. Soon done. But he still went through the dreary motions of a creature that sees some chance of escape.

There was an old man at the next turning, bending to scrabble up scraps from the gutters. Havor called to him. When he turned up his face, Havor saw that he was blind, and something in him chilled and cringed—he had seen so many maimed and crippled in Avillis and her towns, it appeared to him all part of the darkness that was drawing close.

"Do you know of a physician in Arnos, or a herbalist?"

When he asked, the old man cocked his head towards the sound. "A dealer in herbs," he said after a moment, "last house in Southgate Street."

As Havor started to ride on, the old man shrilled, "Alms! Do you have a little coin you're not wanting?"

"Yes," Havor said. "Also I carry the Lord of Avillis' gold Cup, with which he worshipped the Dark, and which I stole from him. Do you still want my coin?"

No one answered this time. When he looked back, he saw the old man groping away, fast as a day-blind worm in terror.

A bitter smile twisted Havor's mouth. He carried a great treasure, but he was safer from robbery than any trader with a few copper bits.

The houses in Southgate Street were crowded close against the southern wail, hovels mostly, with needle-slits for windows and a sullen slum stink blowing over the stained snow. The herbalist's dwelling was one with the rest of the warren, of leaning, lop-sided brown brick, but distinguished by a certain sign hanging from the lintel: a string of yellowing rodent skulls.

Havor tied up the horses to a stake sticking out of the wall, and hoped they would not move, for if they did, it seemed likely that they would pull the house down with them. At the deep recess of the door he hesitated. There was a pane of dull green glass set in the wood, too thick to be seen through, yet out of the cracks in the wood and the brick seeped a weird odor of rank growing things, decayed leaves, compost, and other vegetable reeks, both sharp and musty.

Havor knocked with his mailed fist. The house seemed to vibrate and thunder with the sound. At first nothing appeared to be stirring, but then he caught a faint brightness swelling in crooked whorls in the green glass.

"Who's there?" a voice suddenly rasped from inside the door.

"A traveller," Havor said, "in need of your craft."

The voice muttered to itself. Presently it said, "What is it you need?"

"Let me in, and I'll tell you."

There was a long silence while the creature—man or woman, Havor had been unable to tell from the voice—deliberated with itself. Then the grating of rusty bolts, and the door angled open.

Havor stepped through into a small dark room where the smell of plants and herbs came rushing to greet him in a choking fog. The herbalist, if so it was, was a tiny crouching thing swathed in brown garments out of which poked a shrivelled little tortoise head and tortoise-paw hands, clutching and shielding a single sad candle.

"Well, what is it you're wanting?" it demanded, and as if to show him the wealth of his choice, lifted up the light so that the whole room opened into tilting pallor. Havor glimpsed great mounds of dried weeds, stone urns with grey-green tendrils and pinched flowers spilling out of them, battalions of tall stoppered jars. Up on the wall was hung the polished skull of a stag which, because of the antlers still attached, had a devilish look. Through a low door Havor made out only blackness and the grave-smell of fungus.

"Can you make up a draught to keep a man from sleeping?"

The herbalist crouched lower, and tilted the candle so the harsh thin glare described Havor's face.

"To keep from sleeping? It's usually the other way about."

"Not with me."

"Maybe not. Maybe not."

There was a long pause during which the creature muttered to itself again. Then it asked, "Do you want this draught to commit a crime, or to use on another?"

"Neither. I must keep a vigil three or four nights long."

"And if you doze, what harm?"

"My death," Havor said, simply, as to the priest, and with once more that sense of the irrevocable, the unavoidable.

The herbalist said immediately. "Will you pay me?"

"Yes, if you'll take my payment."

"Why shouldn't I? There's little enough coin in the town. They pay me with their skinny chickens, or their old clothes—or the promise of things that never come."

"I stole and carry the Chalice of the Lord of Avillis," Havor said. "The Blood Cup." Now it will refuse me its herbs, he thought. I should have told it after, or not at all.

But the creature gave a brief trilling laugh.

"Outside," it said, "three horses. I'll make you your draught for two of those. They'll sell for a fine fee sometime. Come now, don't dawdle. It's an absurdly high price, but you're desperate and I'm thrifty and unafraid."

"As you say," Havor remarked, "I want your wares. The horses are yours."

"Sit then, and I'll see to it."

So, for an hour, Havor sat in the acrid gloom while the herbalist pottered and muttered and rattled about among the collection of weeds.

Perhaps this being is a charlatan, Havor thought, and knows no more about herbs than the substance of the moon. I'll pay him, and drink his muck, and it will do no good.

But he had little choice. Besides, the two extra horses were only an encumbrance; he would be glad enough to be rid of them, though what would become of them in the yard of the hovel before they were sold he scarcely liked to think.

Outside, the last of the afternoon drained and waned. He did not see the evening gather, there was no proper window in the room, yet somehow the shadows gave the impression of massing more thickly. The great polished stag's head seemed to swim and gleam, growing whiter as everything else darkened, as if it had a light inside it.

Finally the herbalist came out of the black place with a stoppered phial of murky glass, and inside the glass a fluid resembling tainted ditch water.

"That?"

"This," said the herbalist. "Swallow a sip every few hours, you needn't be too exact. It'll grow less effective the longer you're without sleep, so you'll need to take more. It may not save you. But it's the best I can do."

Havor thanked him. The honesty of the words only confirmed his own doubts, but lent credence to the brew. He was very cold, a dismal dank cold that seemed to chew his very bones.

The herbalist followed him out into the street.

The sky was low and smoky, but garnet-red over the western line of roofs where the cloud mass broke off in a curious line, almost mathematically precise.

The horses shuffled and stamped. Kachil's mare and

Feluce's roan seemed to know their new master. They whickered, and thrust their long noses into the herbalist's robe. Amazingly it produced sweetmeats for them. They would not do so badly, then. Havor was glad to see that, despite the rest.

He mounted and rode away, up the street, and soon out of the south gate of Arnos, and on to the old road.

And now we shall see, he thought. But though he felt no actual fear he did not have much hope either.

Perhaps that, then, was the key to Havor of Taon—acceptance, and a stoical sense of doom.

After a mile or so, he drank half a mouthful of the concoction. It burned his mouth, and soon his eyes felt burning too, and an alert, prickling energy swept over him, like fever.

7. The Snow-Waste

ARNOS HAD DROPPED FROM SIGHT behind him beyond the curve of the hills, and the sky was dark with overcast and evening when the new snow began to fall.

It came light and soft at first, insect wings brushing his face. Then a wind woke up in the hills, in a cave perhaps, as it did in the old stories, and came roaring up across the sloping land from the east. The wind buffeted the snow, set it whirling and spinning, changed its softness into the million points of a knife, and hid the land behind its motions.

For a while Havor rode on, his head bowed against the blizzard. The snow clogged thick around the hooves of the horse. He could see nothing ahead or to either side save the spiralling whiteness, hear nothing but the angry tormented voice of the wind. He lost the sound of the paving underfoot.

Suddenly there was a mass of solid blackness lunging at him out of the snow. The horse shied, but it was only a piece of an old wall.

Havor dismounted, and led the horse under the deep archway of broken stone. Perhaps it had been part of a guard tower like that ivy-smothered ruin he and Feluce had come on. He thought of the old woman slinking out from the tower's mantle, and the ghastly secret she and Feluce had smiled at together. But not for long; it was too cold, too dismal to go over another's death.

The snow spun. It seemed it might spin forever.

A great tide of lassitude broke over Havor as he crouched in the lee of the ruin. He brought out the herbalist's phial and took another small sip. The fire caught at his throat. Presently the wind dropped and the snow fell in straight lines, and then slackened.

He began to make out a white open country with the odd tree or clump of trees standing here and there. The woods had thinned into nothing. Of the road there was no trace.

He looked back, the way he had come.

The whole landscape seemed empty, but it was hard to be sure. Nevertheless his heart began to knock against his chest, as if demanding an answer.

In the blizzard he had lost the road. Could it be that he had somehow lost his dark companions also?

The snow stopped. He left the shelter and looked upwards. The sky was icicled with stars. He would judge his way now, as a sailor, by the lights in the sky, to get to Venca.

A bright hopeful mood, almost a laughing mood, settled on him. But he seemed to be glancing sideways at himself, and he mistrusted this mood as he would mistrust the moods of a stranger.

He led out the horse, and mounted. His head swam slightly as he did so. He caught the pommel to steady himself, and the stars wheeled like comets behind his eyes. But the giddiness left him quickly. He began to ride at an even steady pace over the unmarked white land, heading west by the sky signs.

He rode through the night. Only once did he sip again

from the herbalist's phial. He felt wide awake, as if he need never sleep again, and sure, and purposeful, as if some supernatural protection had come to him. And all the time, in the pit of his brain, there burned one dreary little spark of knowledge, which said, "Mistrust this, for none of it is so. You are not safe, you are not sure, there is no guardian. It is the herbs which make you think this." Still, it was hard to be hopeless just then.

Dawn seemed to come suddenly, sewing hills and clouds together with golden thread. The landscape had not changed; he might have stood still all through the dark. The stars paled and melted but, from the position of the sun, it seemed he was yet making for the west.

He had passed no homestead or farm in the night, and none was visible now. It was a deserted land.

Havor had a sudden uncanny vision of himself and the horse. He saw them as a hawk might see them; two tiny living objects drawn on the frozen sheet of the snow that stretched away and away, empty, on every side.

He felt the horse quivering under him from weariness, and turned its head towards a distant clump of trees which stood out like lead-work against the snow.

Once among the trees he tethered the horse, fed it, and threw over it his own blanket, then cleared the snow and made a fire, and crouched by it, gnawing on a scrap of black bread. He had been uneasy in the open; he had needed the shelter of the trees. The sky seemed too wide over him; he was too perfect a target out on the whiteness of the waste.

He did not want the bread. He made himself eat it. A thick pungent blue smoke rose from the damp twigs in the fire. He shut his eyes against it.

He had not felt tired until then. But as if the shutting of his eyes were some form of signal to his body, a great wave of sleep came rolling in on him.

Well. So he would sleep. The road was gone, and they—he had seen nothing behind him since the snow. He had cheated them of his death last night—besides, the sun was up . . . He let the heavy breakers take him, and carry him out into the murmuring sea.

There was a girl walking over the snow.

She wore blue slippers embroidered with gold, and where they touched the whiteness, they left a sort of colour, a sort of shine. Havor looked at her and into her face. He thought of a candle flame—the white oval center of its heat rimmed by the yellow flickering aureole. In her left hand she carried two switches, one tawny and one white. After a moment he recognized the brush of a red fox, the tail of a white cat. In her right hand she held out to him, like a gift, the long, black-ribbed feather of a hawk, and she smiled.

A knife stabbed into his wrist. He woke instantly, crying out. A piece of burning wood had spat at him and scorched his flesh. He touched distractedly at the hurt, dazed, panting, the sweat running down his body like scalding ice.

No. He must not sleep then. Even here, even by day.

So close. Yet he had not seen her face to know it—only the whiteness, the halo of gold hair—like the candle flame. And her smile.

He drank one fierce swallow from the glass tube. He thought: I've lost the road. Can I trust the direction of the sun to lead me to Venca? Two days off from me, maybe three still, without a guide, and the herb drink half gone already, and the horse tiring.

The skin between his shoulder blades prickled. He turned, looking back. He saw them then. The hopeful mood that had kept him from seeing was gone. Far off, as before, but very clear. Three black horses with pale manes, three black figures, one with a flickering yellow flame about its head. They were quite still, waiting. Three black crows perched on a gallows.

For an instant a half-formed prayer struggled into Havor's mouth. But he could not utter it. Not for himself. For him those words were already drowned by the noise the thong-whip had made, or the sounds of children crying out of hunger or the cold or sheer misery in that grey house of orphans in the far North, eight years ago.

Presently he kicked out the fire and, taking the horse by its bridle, led it on. He would have to keep moving. His head sung. Once, he looked at the Chalice and it seemed the brightness of it was forcing its way out of the leather now, shining through the sack like a lamp. A lamp to light his way into the Dark.

All that day he kept moving. Twice he halted for half an hour or so to rest the horse; at other times he led it. In the afternoon, woods appeared again across the land in a shadowy drift, and in their knotted skirts he found a wide pool and broke the ice for himself and the horse to drink.

As he lifted his mouth from the water, Havor seemed to catch a gleam of eyes from under the surface, but it was two pale stones lying by each other.

There was no trace or indication of the road. He ached with weariness, but it became part of him; he scarcely noticed now that he was weary, he might always have been thus, it was so familiar to him. Near sunset he caught the glint of a long fair hair on his sleeve, and picked it off. He did not look back.

The sun sank, round as a disc of red Northern copper. As the twilight came on, and hung like drifts of purple gauze in the upper branches of the trees, Havor saw Kachil and Feluce standing in the way. But when he came up to them they were only darkness clotted between two twisted saplings.

Havor no longer thought of anything much. His body felt light, yet wooden. He could not seem to judge distance now, or where things lay in his path, so that sometimes he stumbled in the undergrowth over objects he thought he had avoided. And when the stars formed in the sky, he could no longer seem to make any sense of them.

The moon rose, more slender than the night before, and soon after, a great roof seemed to rear up like a python and catch his legs, and he fell.

The fall stunned him. The world reeled and sickness gushed in his belly. He tried to shake it off, but an instant's darkness swallowed him.

There was a window in the dark, a tall thin window, a daffodil window with a delicate lattice work over it. He did not know if it were filled with yellow glass, or faced on to yellow lamplight or yellow sky. In it hung a black moon.

Havor opened his eyes and struggled, gasping, to his feet.

Behind him, the horse whinnied. It puffed steam, dancing, rolling its eyes when he turned to it. He held out a hand for the bridle and noticed a pale hair coiled about his wrist that slipped from him like a snake.

"Come," he called to the horse, croaking, trying to be gentle. "Come on."

He took a step, and the horse flung up its head, its forefeet next. Its hooves seemed vast silver meteors streaking the shadow. Something fell from its body in a dull metallic clashing. The horse swerved with a shrill squeal. Snow burst from its passage as it plunged away into the wood.

Havor ran two or three paces after it, then came to a standstill, holding to the trunk of a tree. The leather sack, and what it contained, lay in the churned-up white by his foot.

He picked up the sack. It was empty of everything but one. And the terrified horse, galloping away into the night, had taken the last of his food, the warm blanket, the flint and tinder with which he made fire. There was little now between him and the snow-waste, and the dark, and what the dark held for him.

For a moment he thought he would let go of the Chalice and leave it lying, but a sudden image burst in his head of the wood crippled and bare, reeking of some nameless plague, a place of vileness and horror spreading out from the golden core, which was the great Cup, until its poison covered the whole landscape. Whether such a thing could happen he hardly knew any longer, yet the priest's words had stayed with him. So he tied the sack across his shoulders, rather as holy books showed sinners carrying the weight of their sins, like a burden, on their backs. And the sack grew very heavy, or he thought it did.

Then he trudged on, not really knowing now where he went, if it was to Venca, or if Venca existed any longer, only understanding, blindly, stupidly, that the hunter was behind him, and he must not be still.

A time passed which had no meaning and no divisions. Then out of the pitch-black, bone-white, silent world soared a wild keening that broke in two, double-noted, and sank back into the void.

The voice of a wolf.

Havor stopped. He lifted his head, alert to catch again the eerie mournful cry. It did not fail him, but rose almost immediately, and over it arced another, thinner howling, and another still. Wolves, then, many wolves. Wolf-pack.

A shudder ran through Havor, but it was a primitive, purely physical thing. In a weird and crazy way, part of him was very glad to hear a living thing give tongue in this dead world, even if now, for sure, he would never reach Venca.

He went on between the trees, and the cries came like the notes of strange hoarse pipes. But they were distant yet.

There was a rise. He came over the top of it, and the trees parted, and there, lying below him, was the pile of a long haphazard building out of which thrust spears of amber light.

An inn—one of the towered inns of the South. He was near Venca, then, nearer than he thought. Perhaps he had lost track of time in the waste. . . .

Breathing in long gasps, he came down over the ridge, staggering a little. Now he felt the cold, now he felt the ache and the fear—it was all crowding in on him because, abruptly, it seemed he might win through.

In the forecourt one of the tall black flame trees was growing. Icicles dripped from its boughs, chiming like glass at his approach. Shafts of light fell on to the snow in ornate fragments out of high windows.

Above the door, from a wrought golden chain, hung a silver cage. Havor looked up at it. It reminded him, dimly, of something he had once seen. On the floor of the cage lay the skull of a large bird with a ruby set in one of the eye sockets.

Havor placed his hand against the door. Inside, rags of a black velvet curtain blew against his face. It was a long low room, brass lit from the huge hearth. By the hearth a thin, red-haired man was standing.

"Welcome, Havor," the man said. It was Kachil.

Havor went closer, near to the leaping fire, but it gave no warmth. He looked down into the flames, and saw the shapes of towers and palaces—it was Avillis that burned in the grate.

"Two nights now," Kachil said. "Two nights you've cheated them. But you can't escape, sir."

"No, my noble captain, you can't escape, not in the waste, not in Venca either."

Havor turned, and saw Feluce leaning elegantly at the other side of the fire, smiling and bowing to him like an actor in a play. Yet a green water weed draggled slimily about his neck, and chips of ice were caught in the folds of his sleeve.

"I'm imagining you," Havor said, "and this house."

"Just so," said Feluce.

"The herb liquor, and lack of sleep," Havor said. "Hallucinations."

Kachil giggled, and turned into a blood-red fox which barked and ran into the fire. Havor looked at Feluce, but Feluce was gone, and a white cat spat at him and arched its back, and melted like the ice.

Havor crossed the room, and went up the stairs, and found himself in a great church of black pillars and tall narrow windows filled with yellow glass. Snow was floating in somehow through these windows, piling up in drifts on the floor. Black snow. Havor bent and ran his fingers through it and it was not snow at all but the feathers of ravens or crows.

On the altar stood the holy circle, but it was cracked across, and before that was the golden Chalice burning like fire, every jewel a blue or white or scarlet sun.

Havor looked down into the black pit under its rim, but it was filled now, up to the brim with dark, dark red.

"No!" Havor said aloud. "I carry you on my back."

The Chalice paled and smoked away.

Havor turned and grasped at the pillars.

"Trees, trees—"

There was a high hollow singing in his head. He shook it, and opened his eyes, and the white empty world was around him again. No inn. Only the waste. And the wolves singing.

He looked over his shoulder. Low on the ground, through the knots of the thickets, he caught a fleck of emerald light. Ember eyes. Wolf eyes. So, that was to be his going, then. One to sickness, one to water, one to the fangs of beasts. Or did he imagine the wolves, too?

He moved ahead a little way and heard a faint rustling in the undergrowth behind him, not too close, perhaps a spear-cast's distance.

He went on, keeping up a listless motiveless trudging. After a while he became aware that there was only one wolf behind him—the others still gave tongue far off. He smelled the wolf-stink, very faint in the cold, but very real. Why did it not attack him? Perhaps it also was unsure, starving perhaps, weak from hunger in this barren land, ill, and outcast from its tribe. Yes, that must be it. Hunting alone, dragging itself after the upright moving thing which meant life to it. It would not come for him yet, then. But it would herd him, cherish him, keep at his heels, and if he fell or stumbled—

He saw himself suddenly as the sick wolf must see him—a kill, meat. And with that came a kind of pity, and a kind of defiance. This thing he could understand, this thing he could resist, forget that other hunter because here was another hunter more immediate.

"So you want me, brother," he said aloud. "You need my flesh."

Not stopping, he took out the herbalist's flask, and tipped two or three mouthfuls down his throat. A quarter of the liquor remained.

"Come on, then," he said to the wolf. "I'll try for the town, and you for me, and we'll see who'll win."

The other wolf cries were dying over the hills. Only the wolf at his heels kept with him with its little rustling and the breath of its smell.

This time the herbs seemed to clear his head. He felt stronger, renewed. Sometimes the moon was like a skull to him, then he named it: *"Moon,"* and it was. Occasionally the wood was full of tall carven pillars, then he thrust his hands against them and said, *"Trees."* Once Kachil leered down at him from the branches, and he heard Feluce caroling, but there was no girl with candle-flame face and hair. The new hunter had come between.

He and the wolf went on. It was a sort of comradeship.

Dawn opened bright cracks in the sky and poured through. The woods dropped behind again.

Havor sat to rest against the bole of a tree. There was no sign of town or village or even one solitary cot. The snow was sun-stained, as if by blood.

"Well, brother," he said to the wolf, "it looks as if you'll win, after all."

As if it understood, the wolf came suddenly slinking out of cover about twenty paces away, and sat down facing him.

He could see he had been right; it was sick. There was a dull dankness on its pelt, and its eyes were milky and lusterless—perhaps it was part blind. Its ruby tongue lolled.

Compassion took hold of Havor. He wished he could have thrown it some food, but presently it got up and came a little way forward, and he must throw a clod of snow instead to keep it off. It ran back, and sat down again.

"Poor brother," he said to the wolf. It blinked. He saw its beauty, for even now it was beautiful.

Soon he rose and walked on. He thought: It must be

very weak, very sick, not to try for me from behind. Perhaps it will. What then? But there was no remedy.

About noon, his steps began to flag. The wind had picked up again, and on the higher ground it screamed and flapped about him.

"Not so long now," he said to the wolf.

He felt nothing. He was not afraid. He would fall, but he had the knife, the knife and the wolf should have him, and it would be too quick for those others to slip in between. There would be no sleep for them to chain him in, merely the long dark that he surmised followed life, which he could only trust would be private for him.

The wind became the thong-whips of the priests. He cursed and grunted beneath the whistling lashes, and then the earth leaped up, and he rolled, and lay facing the great blown tapestry of galloping clouds that seemed like the cavalry of some sky-born army.

Then he saw the wolf standing at his feet. Havor fumbled in his belt for the knife. Quicker, better for both. He was almost glad, if it had to be, that his death would be life for the starving wolf.

"Wait, brother," he said, "one moment more."

And the wolf, startled by his voice, jumped back a pace, and obeyed him.

His hands were so numb that it was difficult to position the knife. And then, when it seemed he had it right, and was ready, there came a burning light across the air which struck the wolf between the eyes.

It made no sound. It spun about, fell, and lay still.

Havor pulled himself on to his elbow. He leaned and touched the wolf. It was warm. Its fur was crusted with the snow, and a knife-hilt stood up from its forehead.

"Poor brother," Havor said. His eyes were abruptly wet with tears.

"I hated to kill it," someone said above him, out of the air, "but the wolf-kind kill to save their own, and you and I are human-kind and must do the same. Besides, he was dying anyway, I think."

Havor lay back again and looked up, too weak to get to his feet.

He saw, he thought, a slender, very young boy, cloaked and hooded for the cold. The boy had a familiar look. Havor remembered firelight, a small bag of money, an anxious voice—Lukon. Lukon who had asked him to bring his pay to his mother's farm; Lukon, because of whom he had taken a share in the Chalice; Lukon, who was dead, and buried by the wall of Avillis.

"You're not real," Havor mumbled.

The boy knelt by him. "I'm real. And you're sick. Did you come far?"

And suddenly, Havor saw it was not a boy but a girl, a girl of sixteen or seventeen years, with a strange, finely made face and eyes the tawny green of acorns, and long hair the colour of malt spilling now out of her hood. She was so unlike any of the visions, her face so unlike the candle-flame face, that he accepted her reality at once.

She took back her knife and cleaned it quickly in the snow, and her face was pale but set and unflinching.

"Come, soldier," she said, "try to get up. I'll help you."

And somehow, for her slightness was very deceptive, she did help, and he was on his feet.

There was a little pony in a clump of trees, with wood piled on its back that she had been gathering. She threw it off, and made him ride, while she led the animal.

"The farm's just over the next rise," she said. "I don't venture far in the winter. It's lucky you spoke when you did or I'd never have found you. Where were you making for? Venca?"

"Yes," he said.

"Well," she said, "you can get warm and eat and sleep at the farm, and then make on. It's only a mile or so."

"All but sleep," he said, but very softly; she did not hear.

They came over the rise, and he looked down and saw a huddle of small buildings—barns and huts and at the center an old house with a scribble of smoke above its chimney. On the west side was a solitary tree, a crippled pine, leaning so far over that its roots were in one place free of the ground.

In Haver's brain a voice said, "You'd know the house by a great crippled pine on the west side."

"Lukon," he said aloud.

The girl hesitated. Not turning, she asked, "Did you know my brother then, soldier, in the King's war?"

"Yes," Havor said. His tongue felt thick. So, it had fallen to him at last to give them what was theirs, that news of death, that cloth bag of coins, if not the consolation and the wealth of the Chalice. The mother and two sisters of Lukon. He had noted the likeness, yet not understood that he had happened on the farm near Venca.

He took out the herbalist's glass and drained it and threw it away into the snow.

There was no help for him in Venca, he knew it. He had thought it would be death with the wolf, but death would still come, even though the wolf had not had him. This respite was for another reason. He had only one thing left to do.

And Lukon's wage. Was it tainted also, now he had carried it? Well, he could warn them. The herbalist had not been afraid to take his horses. Perhaps it made no difference to others, after all, the golden curse he bore on his back.

She said no more to him. Perhaps she guessed her

brother had been killed. He would tell her at the farm, tell the three of them, and give them the little cloth bag.

Then he would take a spade, as once before, and go out and bury the Chalice deep, and sit down by it. And wait for death.

8. Silsi

AS IF HIS OWN BODY understood that this was the final resistance he would demand of it, his head cleared and his blood tingled. He came alive to the cold and the brightness of the day. When he got off the pony in the house-yard his legs seemed firm and strong under him, and there was that deceptive feeling, as earlier, that now he could travel miles, untiring, his mind sharp as a knife. He knew this time that it would not last. But it would last long enough for his purpose, for he did not ask much now.

He noticed that there were no animal sounds about the farm, no cow mooing or pig grunting, no barking dog, and no fowl clattering up at their approach into the yard.

The girl led the pony into one of the little outbuildings, and was back in a moment. She thrust open the timbered house-door, and stood aside for him to enter first, an ancient courteous gesture of the South.

It was bare inside, with only a table and a bench or two, three great chests black with age, and a tall old chair by the hearth. She came after him and lit the sallow lump of wax in the clay lamp, for it was windowless save for a little pane over the door, and very dark despite the red coals fluttering on the fire. She said, with a sort of defiance, "I've not much. But you're welcome to share it with me. My name is Silsi."

"Your mother and sister are from home?" he asked.

"Yes."

There was something about the way she said it, a sort of bitterness that was the mask over something else. He was, at that moment, very sensitive to such things.

"Have they gone far? Will they be back before sunset?"

"Not far, soldier, but they won't be back. There's a grave behind the farm, up on the hill. I dug it myself for them. It was a sickness; many died of it in the Venca villages. They won't be back." She looked at him, and added, "No pity, please. And no words of comfort which you can't mean. They were nothing to you."

"Your brother, Lukon," Havor said softly, "died at Avillis, in the North."

Her face did not alter. She said crisply, "So. I guessed."

She turned and stared at the fire and said, "He would go after the King's war. And what was there to hold him here? The rotten land which gives nothing, and every day grey and like all the other grey days which have gone before. He thought he'd get rich with the army, and make us rich. A dream. But he was very young."

"He sent you this," Havor said, and took the little cloth bag from his belt and laid it on the table in front of him.

She glanced at it, and then up into his face. "And you came all this way to bring it to us?"

"Yes and no," he said. "There was another place I meant to go to first and come here later. But things worked out differently."

He had taken the leather sack from his shoulders and

laid it too on the table. She had not asked about it, and now she was at the fire setting beer to heat.

"My name is Havor," he said slowly. "Havor of Taon, north beyond the Great River. I was your brother's captain for a short while. I don't know how he died, only that he did, and that he wanted very badly for you to have what was in the cloth bag." She did not speak. He went on, still slowly, feeling his way around the words, while the glow and warmth of the old room soaked into him and made him only want to be quiet, fearing nothing in the world. "Before I left Avillis, I helped steal a great treasure. A Cup of gold. I have it here."

"Are you a thief then?" she asked softly. "That surprises me. Were you in need?"

"Of a kind."

She came and set the beer before him, and a platter of bread and cheese. He drank a little of the liquor, but he felt no hunger, though it was almost two days since he had eaten.

"Don't stint yourself," she said, defiantly, as at the door. "I'm not so poor that I can't afford to let you have this."

His head swam, suddenly. The brief horrible giddiness left him shaken and confused. He had not meant to tell her much, but somehow he found himself muttering, "Don't waste your food on a condemned man."

"Condemned? What do you mean? Did you kill, too?"

"Kill? What else is war but killing? But no, Silsi, I don't mean that."

"What then?"

He found she had sat beside him at the table. Her young, fine-made face was full of anxiety, a desire to help despite all her own trouble and sorrow. She had a kind of curiously convincing strength to her that her physical slightness only emphasized.

Looking in her eyes he seemed to see down into the currents of an ocean, very deep and very clear, a depth and clarity created by pain. Her kindness made him want to tell her nothing, to add nothing to what had hurt her already, and it made him in fact tell her almost everything in a few halting, unfinished sentences. He did not think she would understand him, or, if she did, that she would either scoff and disbelieve, or else grow terrified. But she never stirred. Only her face paled a little as it had when she cleaned her blade after the wolf.

"Yes," she said, when he was finished, "such curses are well known to me. I've read of such things."

"Take Lukon's money to the priests at Venca," Havor said, though his lips felt stiff and dry. "Perhaps they can cleanse it for you."

She smiled, a thin, dismissive little smile.

"The priests never helped my family before. Besides, it's a small thing now, compared to the rest. But you never said why you took the Chalice."

"It doesn't matter anymore."

A coal burst on the fire, casting up a spume of sparks that bobbed in the girl's eyes and went out as if that ocean behind had quenched them.

"It's getting dark," he said.

The single pane of dull glass above the door was growing somber; the sun would soon go out and night open its great wings across the east. He seemed to have lost track of time in the farm. No matter. Soon time would stop, his time, at least.

"For us," Silsi abruptly said. He looked at her again. "You stole the Cup for us. Didn't you? Lukon told you how it was here, and when you saw the gold . . . you thought of the money you could bring us, along with the grief—to ease it."

"No," Havor said. "I thought so, perhaps. But there

was some kind of sorcery, even then. I wanted to touch the Chalice, hold it. Don't think I stole it for you. It was a sort of greed all along. The same as Kachil and Feluce."

"No," she said, shaking her head. "I heard you with the wolf, remember. You stole for *us,* not for yourself. I know—it's a gift we had, my kin and I, and I still have it. Lukon knew his death when it waited for him, didn't he? And I know you, Havor."

"Well," he said, "it makes no difference now." And he got to his feet. His whole body ached and protested. Not long, he said to it, as he had to the wolf. Not much more aching.

"Wait," she said.

"For what?"

"Where are you going—what will you do?"

"I'll take a spade from you, if you can spare one," he said. "I'll carry this thing as far as I can, a long way from here. Then I'll dig a hole and drop it in and cover it up."

She glanced at the leather sack. She had not asked to see the Chalice. All the others had seemed to want to see it, even when they were afraid.

"And then?" she said.

"And then."

He went to the door and opened it a way. A gust of bitter air slid in by his legs like a winter beast, and the fire spat at it angrily. For a moment the fire appeared to him to be a great burnished hound snarling on Silsi's hearth to protect her. But he pushed the image out of his mind, and looked instead out across the snow-layered fields.

The sun had gone down already, so cloud-smothered and pale there had been no real evidence of sunset. Everything was blue with evening now, and up in the woods above the slope down which she had led him earlier, he saw them standing: three riders, black against the blue, on their black horses, and about the head of one of them the flame tongues of pale hair greened over by the dusk.

He found the girl standing at his side.

"Do you see?" he said. Somehow it did not occur to him that their nearness could harm her, for they wanted only him.

"I see—something. Shadow, perhaps."

"For you, then, let it stay a shadow; for me it has substance. Can you let me have a spade?"

She hesitated. "Yes."

"Get it now, Silsi," he said. "I want to put as much distance as I can between myself and your farm before I have to stop."

She turned and went away, out of the door into the dusk. All the time she was gone, he stared up at the three on the slope, or the shadow he took to be the three, but they never moved save for that flicker of greengage flame, and soon Silsi was back.

"Here."

He took the rough old spade into his hands. The iron blade was notched and toothed, the haft stained and polished from much handling. Had Silsi, too, used it to make that grave for her mother and sister, on the hill behind the farm?

"Thanks," he said.

She stood back from him, and said coldly, "How far can you go? You're half dead already."

"Far enough. If I start now."

Her mouth tightened. She seemed to come to a swift decision.

"There's a way to travel faster—a track. I can show you."

"No," he said. He didn't want her out in the night with him, and them behind.

"Yes," she said. She snatched up her cloak and was into the yard ahead of him.

"Come," she said, "it's not far off, but we'll have to climb the hill."

Havor followed her.

Shapes were blurred over now; his head thrummed and drummed with each beat of his heart. They passed the crippled pine tree presently. He saw it like something under water, but the visions were in his eyes again, and in his ears. There was a dryad in the tree, crippled like the tree, weeping in her shell of bark.

The hill was glassy with snow. He slipped and scrabbled behind the girl, and once or twice looked back, but he could see nothing very clearly through the purling evening, only one small oval of amber light—the kitchen window-pane of the farmhouse. It grew dimmer and more distant with every difficult step. The last beacon in the world, going out.

He thought he had felt despair before, but he realized at last that he had never come near it. Despair was this aching climb, this frozen toil towards darkness. It was a black weight round his neck, a black burden on his back, a black pit that swallowed him.

Now there's no turning back. The finish comes now. No way out. And no hope of one.

Yes. Here was their key to him, just as with Kachil and Feluce. Consent. Kachil consented in terror, overwhelmed. Feluce consented with joy and expectancy. Havor merely consented, without real fear, certainly without pleasure. But it would be enough.

Suddenly, they had reached the crest of the hill. Havor stood breathing, the girl stood looking up into his face, her own expressionless and white so that it blurred into a snowy paper shape and he could not seem to see her features, only her eyes, so pale, pale green they were like certain gems found in the Eastern lands.

Then the haft of the spade burned in his hand, or seemed to burn, and he looked aside and saw the marker poking up out of the snow.

"Yes," Silsi said, not turning, "they're buried here, my mother and my little sister. I scratched their names on the wood but it will weather and fade. And there's the way."

He shifted his gaze, and saw the track, slightly lower than the ground about it, winding off, uncannily clear to him as something drawn with ink in the snow.

He wanted to say more to her, but he was not sure what. He could not seem to fit words together.

She cried out, "Go on then. Go!"

He thought she was afraid, so he moved aside and took the track, and went along it at a fast shambling pace, leaving her standing alone by the graves.

9. The Dark

THE MOON ROSE some time after. It was not like a skull to him now, but rather a white paper mask hung up in the sky. The wind had dropped. It was very still with only the sound his boots made on the snow.

He followed the track. Over the curving land, over the backs of low hills. At first the land was featureless, but then again there were woods, straining their crone fingers, webbed with white. Once, far off, he saw a glimmer on the horizon, like the thousand lamps and torches of a city glowing up into the night. Venca, perhaps. But he could not be sure. Truth or illusion, it was all one now.

He followed the track. He followed it carefully, afraid of walking in circles, for he did not want to die near to the old farm. But he was half afraid of coming on a village that the track might lead to, imagining again the contagion spreading from the Chalice when he let it drop, and so, at last, maybe an hour later, he stepped aside from the way and into the trees.

Icicles jinked and gleamed about his head, and he seemed to walk very soft. He felt nothing, no cold on his face, no brush of thicket or bite of stone underfoot. Soon he could not feel his legs under him as they moved, and he had to picture to himself each step, each flex and progress and contact with the ground, to stop himself from falling.

Then the ground itself cascaded away in front of him.

He halted and looked down into a jagged wound of snow and black rock; an old quarry, though what material had been gouged from it seemed long forgotten. Nothing came here now, except birds or snakes or other things, by accident, for on its floor, some twenty feet below, lay animal bones half under the white.

He knew the quarry at once, like a homecoming. It was the place he must leave the Chalice. And himself.

Trees clung round the edges. He held to these where he could, and used the spade as a pick and a staff, and managed the first few feet well enough. But after that the slope was bare. He slipped and lost hold of the spade, which rang on the rock and plummeted into the snow of the quarry floor. He crawled a yard after that, then slipped again and felt the hard earth strike his back, after which he was rolling and falling and helpless.

He lay in the snow and laughed a little, for no reason. He was so numb, so without feeling that he could not tell whether or not he had been hurt. But he seemed whole and found he could stand.

The spade had stuck upright in the snow. He pulled it free. Was there any soft ground on the floor? The blade jarred on rock several times, each fruitless impact exhausting him. He noticed there were two or three pale hairs showing up like gold wires on his sleeves. He did not bother to pick them off.

Then the spade bit. He levered, and up came the white top layer and the black undersoil. The Chalice rolled across his back at every movement.

It did not take long, for soon he struck rock again, but

it was just deep enough, just wide enough, the pit he had made. He unfastened the cords, opened the sack. He took out the Cup, and held it in his hands.

Like fire, yellow fire; he could warm all his frozen body at its hearth.

Somewhere, up over the lip of the quarry, out of sight, a sound came like the sound of a hoof on snow.

Havor raised his head. "Yes, my lords and lady," he said, and his voice was hollow and metallic on the icy air, "I'm here. Why not come for me now? No? You can't take me until I sleep, can you? The coward's way."

He let go the Chalice. It fell into the shallow pit, uttering its bell note on the rock at the bottom. Havor toiled with the spade, heaping back the broken snow and cold hard earth. When the hole was covered, he looked down and seemed to see a yellow light shining up through the soil at him.

He thought suddenly, a tree might grow from the Chalice, a golden tree, with gems on its branches. He had thought something similar when he buried Kachil, he remembered. But the leaves of this tree would never fall (sapphire leaves, topaz leaves), and the fruit of this tree would be fires. The diamonds were like swords to his eyes, the rubies like blood . . .

Somewhere, up over the lip of the quarry, out of sight, a sound came, like a sighing wind.

"Yes, yes," Havor whispered, "impatient undead. You must wait a little longer."

He found a loose rock, and dragged it over to the place where he had buried the Chalice, and laid it there, then another and another. As the rocks grew smaller they seemed to grow heavier. Soon he had built a mound like a little altar over the pit. (He imagined the tree thrusting out sinuous golden coils, like serpents, up through the skin of earth, pushing the rocks aside.)

There had been an old story—a king's son fought a giant and stunned him and bound him, and then, by means of magic, pulled down a mountain over the giant's cave, to keep him in.

"Now I need a mountain," Havor said.

Where had he heard this story? A night in the orphans' house, perhaps. There had been one child who told stories . . .

Somewhere, up over the lip of the quarry, a sound like a shadow, breathing.

Havor lay down on the freezing ground, and did not feel the cold, only the cold in the core of his soul.

What next? he thought. Sleep next, he thought. And then they come. No more resistance, no more pain. A meeting in the dark.

He shut his eyes. At once the great sea of sleep came surging towards him. He saw it, in his brain, the huge black glistening waves, spume-capped with a confusion of clamoring dreams.

He had no faith. The priests had killed it. Yet oddly, now, in the last moment, without any hope or entreaty, without really any conscious reason, he found himself speaking a child's prayer, that child he had been eight years before in the North, that prayer uttered in misery and total loneliness.

"Oh, my God, whatever my sin or sorrow, deliver me from the night and the darkness of the night, arm me against fear, and shield me from evil, and bring me safe to the morning."

Then the tall waves bore down on him, and covered him, and the breakers clashed in his head and drowned him, and he was lost on the wild ocean.

The road. He was on the road.

On every side ran the snow, dead white, but the road

was whiter. It was dark, but dawn was coming, for there was a bright flushing on the edge of the sky.

He was riding, not the horse with dun hair, but a creature made of night and snow, all black with a moon-white mane and tail, the skin of which felt shiny-cold to him as if it were made from polished stone.

Clouds were blowing up the road, though the sky was clear. They wrapped about the horse's feet, and unwrapped and fled on, black clouds, rushing without a wind.

The horse came up and over a rise, and there, ahead of him, a company waited for him on the way.

Black banners. Three black horses with pale manes stood stone-still and stared at him. They drew a black hearse that carved out its shape on the lightening sky. Over it hung a black velvet canopy with a gold device, and at each corner stood an iron torch pole, spitting green flame from its crest. On the canopy's rim perched a raven, making no sound.

Two men and a woman stood at the horses' heads. The men were all black, hooded, gauntleted, and on the thin fingers of the gauntlets glittered topaz and diamonds, but in the eyeholes of their hoods glittered nothing, only shadow. The woman, too, wore black, and a black veil wound about her head, but her face and her shoulders and her hands were bare, and white as wax. She wore no jewels, no rings, but she had eyes—gold fringed eyes with irises as black as jet.

Why are they like this? Havor thought, she whole, the father and the brother bones? Yes, they burned, the Magus and his son; she smothered in the smoke, and died before the flames had her. This is how they remember themselves beyond the grave, so this is how they are.

He thought all this very rationally, yet his heart thudded in leaden beats of slow, cold terror. He seemed to be two men at once, the victim and the observer.

The horse he rode came right over the rise, and Havor found himself close enough now to look down into the woman's face. She was very young, only a girl after all. He felt a curious wrenching of pity because she had been corrupted so early and died so young. Then he found that he and she were riding side by side on the white-maned horses, the hearse rolling behind. Havor stared at her profile and thought: She isn't real. Only a dream.

He said to her aloud, "You're my nightmare. You don't exist. How can you harm me?"

But she answered nothing, and his words seemed to have no substance or reality themselves, and he saw that, being bound by the laws of the dream-place, he was also vulnerable to it.

Then he looked at her slim hands and noticed that the nails had grown long and curling as claws, as nails are said to go on growing for a time on the hands of a corpse in the tomb, and this made him shrink in an absolute horror, for she was undead, and could not be reasoned with any more.

The hooves of the horses struck up sparks from the paving. Havor realized that the dawn was fixed on the horizon, but it was on the wrong side of the sky. Presently he saw it was a city burning in the distance: *Avillis.*

They came to a tall tower, very old, yet not fallen though part of the wall was gone, which stood up like a jagged black rent in the flame-ribboned sky. All the horses stopped. One of the hooded men—father? brother?—came to help the woman to dismount.

Such courtesy among the dead, Havor thought. They carry court manners into the Dark. But it occurred to him that perhaps they had loved each other a good deal, these three, whatever else they had done in the world, and there came again that twist of compassion. Fool, he thought. Fool, they'll kill you soon. Don't pity them.

He found he also had dismounted. He did not remember doing so. There seemed now to be frequent small gaps between one thing and the next, as in an ordinary dream. There were stairs inside the tower. He went up them and the woman went ahead; he heard the rustle of her dress, and there was a weight across his back, like the burden of death. Sometimes they passed narrow window slits, showing the far-off fires of the burning city.

At the top of the tower was a long, wide, open place. He could smell smoke. Directly above there were clouds now, whirling and reeling, a dark, muddy green. It seemed all sky, all space; it made Havor giddy. Out of the giddiness and the clouds something grew, and the hearse was somehow on the tower-top with them. The raven screeched and flared its wings. It held a bone in its beak.

Havor looked at the bone, fascinated. The bone of a man? The bone in the raven's beak spun, then pointed down into the ebony coffin underneath, for it was a finger bone. Havor followed the bone's direction; he stood by the casket, and stared in. First he saw Kachil, but his hair was fire, and fever flames danced under his skin. Next he saw Feluce, looked straight into the open eyes, and there were fish swimming in them as if beneath a still, glassy pool. Lastly Havor saw himself, laid out neat and silent, like a marble figure on a tomb.

Havor looked up, and they were waiting, a little distance in front of him, where the tower fell away. There was a block of stone standing up before the broken wall, and on the block a great cup, not gold but black, and out of it rose a thin scarlet smoke.

The woman beckoned but the two men stood immobile.

Havor began to walk towards them.

I have no choice, he thought, I buried the Chalice, and there it is. The red smoke will blind me, and the woman will touch me, and her touch will burn. I shall fall from the tower's head to be smashed on the ground below. That, then, is to be my death.

Part of him knew that he had dug the Chalice up, and climbed the side of the quarry with it, not the stairway of the tower, and that he would fall down on to the rocks, not the hard paving of the pagan road. But it scarcely mattered. He would die anyway.

The black Chalice seemed very big on the sky. The smoke smelled of incense. The woman took his hand in hers. Her hand was very small and cold. A viper coiled in her veil.

They were at the edge of the tower. Below, the ground wheeled.

The woman let go his hand.

Now, he thought.

He thought the skeleton hands would come instead, to push him over the rim. Nothing came.

Havor turned and looked back.

The smoke—it must be the smoke, that made him see six figures on the tower, instead of three—

Under the roiling green vortex of the sky the veiled woman, the two hooded men, black and gold and white. But behind them, three more, very faint, pale as steam, yet hardening . . . Havor stared. A young man, a woman in her middle years, holding by the hand a little girl of nine or ten. They had no colour, no detail, but at their back there was a curious kind of shadow, a sort of opening, in the cloud.

The golden-haired woman half turned her head. The jewelled serpent hissed about her throat. She snarled like an angry leopard. In the markets of the East, animal in cages had snarled like that when they saw the whip that ruled them. The two hooded figures, the Magus and his son, fell back a step. The smoke poured from the

Chalice, making a scarlet column which seemed to uphold the cloud.

Havor began to tremble. He fell to his knees because he could no longer stand. He saw that the three of Avillis were uncertain, disrupted. What do they fear? he thought. Those others, who stood against the sky, pale as milk?

Havor's eyes burned, trying to make them out—a woman with braided hair, a little maid with—yes, with a rag doll on her arm, he could just see it—a young boy in Southern link-mail, a sword in his belt—

"Lukon!" Havor said.

A streak of white light darted over the mark on the sky behind them. Tears ran from Havor's eyes and down his cheeks, molten tears, whether of gladness or terror or despair he could not be sure.

"Dead Lukon," he choked out, "buried at Avillis. And the mother of Lukon and the little sister, dead of a plague at the old farm where the pine tree leans—"

This time the spasm of light opened up the shadow. Havor saw a hollow, a chasm, behind the cloud.

Somewhere, in the earth under him, there came a shuddering shift. A piece of the tower crumbled and broke off under Havor's left hand. But he leaned forward, staring.

The smell of incense and smoke had changed to a stink of burning stuff, the odor of carrion. On the hearse canopy the raven flew up suddenly and melted in a gust of black vapor, and the hearse itself faded; the canopy blew sideways and fell in a stream of black ash.

The Lord of Avillis' golden-haired daughter screamed.

It was not in any way a human sound. It had none of the thrilling awful anguish of a woman's voice. It was rather the howl of a beast cheated of its kill—savage, frightful, desolate.

The colorless figures came drifting up across the tower top. As they drew level with the Chalice the smoke sank down, but they seemed to expand, to billow like gauze, and their white billowing reached out and caught about the Magus and his son and his daughter, wrapped them in fleecy ropes, enveloped them. In that fog Havor saw yellow hair glow and swell and then extinguish like a candle.

Now there was only a great, tumultuous, twisting, curdled cloud on the tower before him, grey and white, that writhed and struggled, and was swept back towards the chasm in the sky, and was drawn through to its last fiber.

Havor, kneeling on the edge of the tower, saw that the sky was empty. Slowly he turned his head, looking for the Chalice. Where it had stood was now a cage of bone, and in the cage a formless thing that dazzled and went out.

Then the world juddered and tumbled. The rim of the broken wall gave way under him. Havor felt himself sliding down the air, and the air was solid, though slippery, like glass; he could not keep hold of it. At the bottom of the air was one last black cloud, which opened its muffled jaws and swallowed him.

Inside the cloud there was no time at all, and on the other side of the cloud was a thread of silver that warmed and widened as Havor opened his eyes into an enormous, wind-brushed, opal sky. A sky of the world, not dream, tinged now with the soft rose-gold of the true dawn.

I'm alive, he thought at once. There could be no mistaking it. I'm alive and whole.

Everything was there in his brain, ready for him, crystal clear. He remembered all of it, from the first moment of his conscious life, to the last second of his fall through space—he had lost nothing, paid nothing, to wake up alive in the new day.

He turned a little, wonderingly. He lay halfway down the quarry side, caught in the arms of a thorn tree, which now cradled him and held him secure. The floor of the quarry was littered with bits of rock and grey mounds of mixed snow and soil that had plunged away under him, but he lay in the tree's strong twisted grasp, unbroken. He leaned back and rested quietly, letting the images and thoughts drift across the surface of his mind.

I never imagined I'd see this dawn.

There was a great peace on him; like a man made well after a long sickness.

Gradually the golden blush filled up the wide bowl overhead, and turned a brazen yellow on its eastern rim. The sun was rising below the head of the quarry, opening the cloud with spokes of light. An embroidery of birds stitched itself across those crocus shafts, unravelled itself behind, and was gone.

Havor stirred and gently disengaged himself from the tangled embrace of the thorn tree.

He had felt no fatigue, until now, when he began to climb back up the side of the quarry, gripping the bare rock in his hands. The weakness came abruptly, but it carried no fear with it.

Soon, he thought, you can rest. With the conviction he seemed to grow strong again, and he came to the top, crawling, grinning, got over the broken place, and stood up.

The morning sun had cleared the horizon's rim. Lying in its path was something small and charred, as if by the sun itself.

Havor bent and touched the thing. It was a goblet, carved from wood, set round with glass gems that had become cloudly and splintered. At some time a fire had licked and mouthed it black.

He had buried the Chalice, and heaped up rocks to cover it, and this, this was only some cheap drinking cup, and yet—Havor knelt on the cold ground, the sun burning on his fingers as he held the cup. He did not know if this were what the Chalice had become when the dark spell was gone from it, or if the Chalice had always been this misshapen trumpery thing, and the spell had blinded all of them to see it differently. He remembered how light it had been to raise, despite its size and metal, so light a girl might have lifted it, and perhaps one had . . .

The cup fell out of his hand and cracked open on the snow, and the splintered glass gems rolled out of it like tears.

Havor turned. There was a girl standing facing him, among the trees, but a dark-haired girl, with acorn green eyes.

"You're safe then," she said.

"As you see," he said. He did not move. He said, "And so, you're a witch, too, Silsi."

"I know the old ways. There's nothing evil there, only strange, and not even strange when you know it."

"How?" he said.

"I spoke certain words above the graves," she said. "I whispered to them what you had done, and why."

"And they came," he said, "your brother, your mother, your sister—the child carried a doll—"

"She had it when she died," Silsi said. "I put it to rest with her, to bring her some comfort. I'm glad it does."

"So they came," he said. "But why could they save me?"

"Because they were three in number, like those that followed you, and they too died in pain—but without wickedness. Because you had no greed for the Cup, and they were your witnesses to that. Also, because the things of the Dark cannot bear pity, and you pitied them, and by pitying them, made them, in a way, human again, and therefore less than they were. But most of all because you are as you are, Havor. There are certain laws, even by night."

She stood quite still, looking at him, and he seemed to understand her very well, as if they had known each other all their lives, she in her loneliness, he in his.

"Come back now," she said. "There's a fire burning."

He pictured the old farm, the crippled tree, the amber light in the little window that he had last seen going away, and it seemed like home to him, as nothing had ever seemed before.

"Later," she said, "you can go on to Venca."

He smiled at her, and she at him, and he went down the track to meet her, and together they turned homewards, easily, as if aware that afterwards he would not be going away.

On the path the black cup lay smashed.

Presently the sun darkened and the wind rose, and the blue-white dust of the snow came down. And when the snow had spread and combed its thick pale hair across the land and the trees, there was no longer any black cup.

Later, the moon rode up the clouds, and shone on the place with a fierce, cold, shadowless light.

The Winter Players

1. Sea Grey

THE WINTER SEA WAS COLD and grey as the voices of the gulls that flew over it, but where it entered the bay before the little shrine, the water turned to a sour vinegar green. Most of the lower steps that led down from the wall of the shrine to the water were also green, dark as slabs of raw emerald, for the sea covered them at high tide. When the storms came, waves would smash over the wall of the shrine, into the courtyard beyond.

A girl stood on the lower steps in the windy afternoon, drawing up her nets to reckon what the tides had brought her. In one net there was a fish. She shook it back into the water. She had no need of it, for the villagers sent her food. She gathered the shells and odd wandering debris of the ocean. Once there had been a rotting pouch with tarnished coins in it—the wealth of a drowned man, or an offering cast from a ship to the demons of the sea.

Today there were no coins.

The girl's hair was a smoky, ashen bronze. She held it from her face with one hand as she examined the shells and placed them in her basket. She would paint them with strange swirling designs and give them to the villagers when they came. They liked to have them, thinking them lucky once she had handled them, since she was the Lady of the Shrine, the priestess. Presently she let down the nets again, and started back up the stairway.

Her name was Oaive, or so they called her, a name like the sound of the sea. She was seventeen years old, but she had been chosen before her birth. One day she would have to choose her own successor, by a secret method written in the Book of Lore. But this was not her problem yet, nor would it be for a long while, until she became old or she fell sick.

Oaive was of the fisher-people. Her mother had cared for her, and taught her to read and to weave. But she had shown her daughter no love, whether she felt it or not. A woman who knew she must lose her child was a fool to love it or make it love her. Oaive's father had perished in the sea several months before she was born.

Oaive learned early on that she was different. The children never added her to their games, and they were never rude to her. Even when she was a baby they looked at her as if she were full-grown. Neither was she given chores, as were the other girls. She went to the shrine instead, to be instructed by the priestess.

The priestess was almost ninety years of age. Her flesh was pleated and then repleated on the pleats. Her eyes were pale and moist as fish-skin. Her body creaked when she moved. At first Oaive had nightmares about her, and about the somber stone place with its doors of iron. Later, she grew used to these things. She accepted her lot, as the beast accepts the yoke.

Finally, when she was fourteen, the priestess had shown her the hidden room where the Relics were. The Relics were inexplicable, holy, secret. None but the priestesses might look at them. One was a Ring, one a Jewel, one a short, narrow Bone. Each had its aura. Once Oaive had seen them, the priestess began to teach her the Mysteries of the shrine.

After that, a great change took Oaive. She had never felt affection for the ancient woman, but now she sensed a bond uniting them, the bond of continuance which the shrine made. It came to Oaive that she was not beneath a yoke; she was the guardian of the people. She stood between them and God. She was glad at last that she would never court or wed, or bear children, never huddle warm among her folk as the flocks of the sheep-people huddled on the chill slopes. She did not belong to the flock. She was the shepherd.

At the end of that year, when Oaive was fifteen, the priestess died, and Oaive became the priestess.

The wall of the shrine was built of stones. The shrine itself stood at the center of the courtyard which the wall enclosed. A platform ran around the outside of the wall, leading from the seaward stairway to the great doorway set in the western side of the wall. When she had come around the platform to the door, she found one of the fisher-people there before her. He was a boy of about thirteen, already sea-hardened as a barnacle. He nodded respectfully to her.

"Greeting, lady. The Elder sent me. A stranger has come, to visit the shrine."

Over the boy's head, the winter sun was getting low on the hills, and heavy cloud made another hill-line behind the first. There would be rain before night.

"A stranger? It's an ill time for journeying."

"Yes, lady. So the Elder said, but the stranger laughed—he said it was his penance to travel in winter—a priest laid it on him, beyond the mist."

"Beyond the mist" meant the unknown terrain inland, where none of them had ever ventured. Sometimes men did come from this direction, over the hills and rocky heights, through valleys where, they said, smoking waters poured like upturned witches' cauldrons into the rivers below. Occasionally in summer weather, travellers had even crossed the sea to seek the shrine. But all such were rare. There had been two in Oaive's time, one for each year of her priesthood.

"He is in the fisher-village, then?" Oaive asked the boy.

"Yes, lady. Since noon. He's like no man I ever saw before—" the boy burst out, worried and intrigued at once, and eager to tell. "He wears a cloak made from a black wolf, and the head is on it still, and the claws. He said he killed it himself. He has a long, long shiny grey knife at his side. My father says it's a sword. His teeth are very white, but his hair is the colour of—of the knife itself, like an old man's hair—but he is young. And his eyes are grey, too—"

"Well," said Oaive gently, "when will he be coming to the shrine? At sundown?"

"At sundown, if you permit."

"Yes. Go now and tell him. Take my greeting to the Elder."

The boy bobbed, and turned and ran back down from the headland towards the fisher-village.

At sunset, as at dawn, Oaive spoke the Ritual in the shrine, and those who came there wished generally to be included in it, and perhaps to burn an offering.

A cold wind was stirring from the hillside. Oaive felt it pass like an omen. She had been trained to know such things, both external signs and those signs she felt within herself. From the moment the boy spoke of the stranger, she had been uneasy. A young man with an old man's hair, and a sword at his side. She did not believe the story of a penance. Why should he lie?

The shrine was bleak in the sinking light. She crossed the yard and entered the priestess's place at the far end of the court.

It was a single chamber, windowless and shadowy. She did not mind the shadows, she knew them. She noted, as ever, the narrow bed scattered with luminous drying shells. On a shelf, in clay vessels, were draughts and unguents she made for the villages; the Book of Lore instructed her on the proper seasons for the gathering of herbs, or the wild sea-wrack from the beaches. Beneath the unlit hanging lamp stood her loom, a damson-dark cloth growing on the frame.

She put down her basket, and lit the lamp. She began to weave, hands and feet busy, thoughts running free.

She could do nothing yet. Her instincts had warned her, well and good. Now she must wait and see.

The rain fell just before sunset, as the sky was deepening beyond her door.

She was tying off the thread of her weaving, for it was almost time for her to go to the shrine. She heard the rain, and looked up, and there in the doorway a man was standing.

She was not sure how long he had been there; the shadow before the rain, his shadow across the threshold were all one. The lamp lit up the loom, not the man, and the cold sky was behind him.

"Good-eve," he said, quietly. His voice was a young man's voice right enough, but bold and sharp as a flint, ready to scratch. "Will you tell me where I might find the priestess?"

"She is here," said Oaive.

"You?" He let out a mocking oath, one she did not

recognize, though the village men had several. "I beg your pardon, holy-lady, but I never thought I'd find you at such ordinary woman's work."

"Has it ever been then," she said gravely, "that you find things always as you thought them?"

He laughed. She liked the laugh, and did not like it. It made her want to laugh also, and she mistrusted him. She rose and trimmed the lamp and angled it a fraction as she did so, and the light reached his face at last.

He was as the boy described him. He looked almost familiar. Lean as a wolf himself in his wolf cloak. The wolf mask had two white gems set under the brow-ridges that flashed like life. The rest of his garments were grey, as if to match the blade at his side and his long hair which shone like the winter sea, and his eyes like bits of mirror. He smiled. His teeth were white and sharp as his voice.

"Am I as they told you, lady?"

"They did not tell me your name," she said.

"Oh. If you want to name me, call me Grey, for my hair."

"Are you afraid to give me your true name?"

"It is my penance, lady," he said solemnly. "I may not give it."

She knew he was lying, but she did not say so.

She took up her shawl.

"It is now the time of the sunset Ritual, if you will follow me to the shrine. Is it blood you wish to be cleansed of, or something else?"

"I have heard," he said, "that there are things in the shrine which will heal wounds, cure ills, lift curses. Did I hear right?"

She guessed then. Fear gripped her like a hand. "Faith will do all this," she said. "You must have faith." She drew the shawl over her head and went out into the rain. He came after at once.

A smolder of brightness on the hills showed the sun's going. The rain fell in straight shafts like the hunter-people's fletched arrows.

She passed under the arch of the shrine and on into the rectangular space beyond. Reddish lights burned in niches. The altar slab stood at the room's end. It was black with the fire of offerings and the Ritual fire, made every dawn and sunset. Three iron doors were set in the wall behind the altar.

The shrine smelled of fish-oil from the lamps, of dank stone, rusty iron, smoke and the sea.

"Well," he said, the stranger at her back, "it's modest. Where do the doors lead?"

"To other rooms," she said. "Please don't speak again to me, until I tell you. I must begin the prayer."

"Very good, priestess," he said most humbly, and once more she sensed his scorn. He was older than she was, and older in deeds, too, as much as years. She was aware of this merely by instinct.

"You must stand at the altar," she said. "Think of nothing, or of God."

"With my eyes shut," he promised, "and my heart open."

She left him by the stone slab and went to the central door. She felt him watching her as attentively as the cat watches a mouse. There was a wheel on the door. Only she knew how many turns to give it, and in which directions. These actions were hidden from him by her own body. The door swung open.

The small chamber beyond was pitch-black, yet she was familiar with it from long use, as the blind are familiar with their own regions. She went to the chest and took the utensils from it and the pot of incense. She carried them out to the altar and arranged them in the proper pattern.

Then she did the magic thing, one of the Mysteries of the shrine. She did not do it to cause fear, though it caused fear in some, but only because it was part of the Ritual.

She called fire. She called it from her own self.

The heat began in her right shoulder blade and ran along her upper arm and whorled in her elbow. As the fire swelled in her forearm, the skin glowed and became transparent, showing the red blood and the bone structure under the flesh. Then the fire ran into her forefinger and she let it drip free upon the altar. It flared up in pale darts, and the incense she had scattered there smelled sweet.

The stranger's face showed nothing, but his eyes were wide as a cat's eyes. If he had had a cat's ears, they would have been laid flat along his head.

Oaive spoke the whole Ritual then. It was not lengthy.

Whenever she had said it in the past, a sort of silence and serenity had come over her. These prayers were so old, only the priestesses understood them, for they were in the same antique tongue as the Book of Lore. Yet today their power did not enfold Oaive. She recited, but her mind was elsewhere. The presence of the stranger was like a cold air.

Presently she said to him, in the way of the Ritual: "Speak now. Tell me what you wish."

"A blessing and absolution from my penance."

"Do you crave these with a whole heart?"

"Oh, yes," he said, "but there's only one thing that can help me."

The hair stiffened on her arms and the nape of her neck. She asked: "One thing. What thing?"

"A fragment of Bone," he said softly, looking straight in her eyes. "Only the Bone can give me peace."

If she had not guessed before, she could not miss now.

"What do you mean?" she asked, to see how he would go on.

"The Relic. The Thing of the shrine. You must be acquainted with it, lady. In far lands they called this the House of the Bone. That is what I was sent to find."

She said slowly: "If there are Relics, they are secret."

"One is a Bone."

"They are secret."

"No."

She was frightened, but must not let him see it. She held herself still and said: "I will say the prayer for you, which is the custom. This is the sum of what I may do. Do you wish to offer? A piece of your hair or of your clothing is the usual offering."

"I will offer silver," he said, "to you personally, if—"

But she began the prayer suddenly, before he had finished. The phrases were dust in her mouth, they nearly choked her.

He kept quiet till she stopped. Then he said: "I have no offering, unless you let me see the Bone. That's all that will help me. I told you that."

"You told me lies," she said.

"In that case, I have no offering, priestess."

He looked at her one moment more, his eyes gone white as the wolf skin's gemstone eyes—the only thing that told her how terrible his anger must be. After this he turned and strode from the shrine, the sword clashing against the doorpost as he went.

One was a Ring of ancient greenish metal. One was a colorless, brilliant Jewel. One was a tiny slender Bone, the length of her finger-tip, smooth with age and handling.

They were said to be miraculous, and they had a feel of miracles, and of stranger things, too.

No one but the priestess knew of the Relics.

They were kept in a box of black wood in the secret room. The room lay below the chamber where the incense was stored, behind the iron door with the wheel. Each priestess took her novice to the room before teaching her the Mysteries of the shrine. The Relics were never given a history, never explained. Their explanation was lost in time.

No one but the priestess knew of the Relics.

No one.

Yet *he* knew, the grey-haired man with the wolf's head on his shoulder.

How? What did he want?

He had gone striding out into the rain, but would he be coming back?

She stood alone in the shrine, her hands pressed flat on the surface of the altar.

Shortly, the rain stopped. The night was falling like another, darker rain.

He came back at midnight. She was not sleeping, for she had been expecting him. He came silently as a thief, for he was a thief, yet she heard him.

The door in the wall about the shrine was shut and barred. The wall of stones was treacherous and high. Still, he climbed up the wall and over it. It would take more than the wall to stop him. She had secured the door of her chamber, too, though she did not think he would come there, and she had been right. His soft footfalls went on across the courtyard to the shrine. It was a blind night, the moon long down.

She waited. Suddenly he cried out, and next came a

string of muffled profanities. He had found what she had left there.

There was no door to the shrine. When the sea leapt across the wall it would pummel in over the floor. But there was a trick to close the way to creatures of flesh and blood.

She had murmured before the open archmouth, an hour after sunset. She had called the shadows, and hung them across the arch like curtains, and seemed to set them burning in hot black tongues.

It was another knack the old priestess had taught her, to call shadows, to make them seem to burn.

Perhaps an ordinary thief would have fled. He had watched her make fire in the Ritual, now he met this: he had seen what she could do. But he did not fly. She had known he would not.

She felt him stand there before the shrine. Not stupidly, not wondering what he should do. He was gathering himself. After a while she heard him speak.

"Shadows don't burn," he said. Nothing more, but it was enough. He grasped the fact that he could overcome the illusion by not believing in it, and he had schooled himself not to believe. She sensed the flames going out in smoke, and she knew he went by the smoke into the shrine.

She was brimming with a peculiar, sad fearfulness, but she unfastened her door and went out to the shrine. She crossed the threshold where even the smoke had faded. Though he had walked soft, she walked more softly, and he did not hear.

He was on the other side of the altar, before the central door. Yet only she knew the correct turns of the wheel. If he had tried it, he surely had lost heart.

When he stepped back from the door she thought for

a moment that he had, but instead he called quietly: "Old door, old wheel, you know the way you must turn. How many times have they turned you, the witch-women of the shrine? You remember. You know. Turn then. I will make you do it."

Oaive shrank inside herself. He understood, she realized, the logic of sorcery, and had the concentration of mind to put his understanding to use. She had half-guessed this from the beginning; now she was positive. He was armed with as much magic as herself, and maybe more.

And the iron wheel was starting to obey him. Slowly, rustily, unwillingly, it was turning.

So she called on the deepest reserves within her. She summoned up a sort of psychic cloak to cover herself—an Aura. It made her appear far taller than she was. It clad her in a fierce unglowing light as if lamps blazed in her skin and eyes. It made her feel invincible, but it would drain her, this power. She could not maintain it long. It was really the last chance she had against him.

The wheel had reluctantly completed its turns. The door hung open, and he had entered the place beyond.

Oaive followed him. When she reached the door, he was already searching for the secret room.

Her unshining brightness flooded the chamber, and he spun round and stared at her. For a second then, she saw he was unnerved.

"You have abused the shrine," she said. Her voice had taken on a sound of dry striking crystals—almost, it made him flinch. "Go," she said, in the terrible auramantic voice. "You will need many years to work off the curse you have already invited."

Another man would have run howling. Not this one. He shuddered, but more as if he were shuddering off his unease than from fright.

"Don't meddle, lady," he said. "I see you gleaming there like phosphorus, and your head near touching the roof and your eyes like daggers. But I recall quite well you're merely a girl whose crown comes no higher than my chin. You've put on your witch-look to frighten me. It does not. I don't believe in your curses. There's only one thing scares me, and that's not here."

She held the Aura steady. She said: "Go, or there will be worse."

"Let there be. I want the thing I told you of. I would have dealt courteously with you, paid you if you had agreed. But no. So, I am a robber. The secret way isn't in the walls, so it's in the floor. Yes. I see your eyelids flicker. It's in the floor. Good."

He knelt, ignoring her. He found the uneven panel almost immediately.

She felt the Aura sinking. She could not hold its tension. She seized the last of it like a spear. She lifted her arm, ready to cast the failing power at him, to stun him. She could summon purely physical help from the villages before he could recover—

But he had jumped to his feet, startling her, and her grip on the bolt of energy faltered.

"Very well," he said, "if you want to fight. Sword for sword, my girl."

And he was gone. At least, the *man* was gone. In his place there stood a pale nightmare: a silver wolf with eyes like dying venomous moons.

Just for an instant she glimpsed it, just until, rising up, opening its salt-white jaws, it breathed on her a breath as cold as snow, and with one paw smote her backwards into night.

2. Grey Wolf's Running

SHE CAME TO HERSELF in the hour before dawn, and her head ached. For a little she could not recollect what had happened. Then memory returned to her, everything.

She got to her feet. A lamp was glimmering near her, which showed the stairs leading down into the secret room below.

He had been there, of course. The wooden box was on the topmost stair, open. The lamp caught the flash of the Jewel, the dull polish of the Ring. He had left the lamp for her, so she could see at once that these two things he did not want and scorned to take. Only the Bone was gone.

She felt a sense of failure and loss that was hard to bear. She needed to weep, to ask someone to aid her. But she was unused to shedding tears, or to seeking counsel or comfort. She was the priestess. She was alone.

Oaive moved slowly across the shine, out of the doorway into the court, and presently from the court to the platform above the bay. The sky had cleared, but the stars were paling. The sea had shrunk away from the coast.

Everything was lightless, formless, sounding faintly of wind and waves.

She thought: If I never tell of it, who will know? The priestesses examine the Relics, no other. But she remembered how he had said that even in far lands they called the shrine the House of the Bone. Or had that been another lie, like the lie of his very person? Man, or beast? After all, if God might be found under the holy roof, what need for relics, mysteries, symbols? Yet there was this dreadful emptiness inside her, as if he had stolen part of her own self. What did the Bone mean to him, grey man, grey wolf, that he must steal to have it?

She debated. She tried to see what she should do. Even the Book of Lore could not help her. There was no mention in it of theft or shape-changing or demons.

Eventually the sky began to widen with dawn over the ocean. The red sun made its road on the sea as if sparks were kindling on the pewter water. Six or seven small boats, black against the sunrise, stood a few miles out; the vessels of the fisher-people, taking up the last catch of the night.

Oaive turned. She looked inland. Each of the nearer hills was dimly colored by the dawn, but the farthest were dark still. The sheep would be stirring there, and the shepherds, and the hunter-people, too, with their dogs, seeking deer before winter locked the woods in ice.

Each year they prayed that the winter would be mild, kind to them, yet even mild winters were harsh on this savage shore. Food grew scarce, the people died.

And this winter, she thought. Who can reckon, since a third of their luck has been snatched from the shrine?

She knew then. It appalled her to know, but she was also elated, for she saw her path, evident as that sunpath on the sea.

Quietly and deliberately she began to speak the Ritual, there on the headland. She did not call fire. She had no incense. When the prayers were done, she walked towards the fisher-village.

There were three Elders, one from each village. They sat in the communal long-hall of the fisher-people, and the rest of the folk had come crowding in as soon as they heard the priestess had summoned them. It was almost noon.

There were no windows in the long-hall. Fish hung from the beams to smoke in chains of blackened silver. Torches and fires dispersed a hot yet cheerless light without much warmth.

Most of the men were older than Oaive, and the Elders were very old, yet she felt none of her youth before their years. She felt older than any of them, for the centuries of the shrine were on her.

She had told them of the thief. She had not told them of his magic. They would guess him a magician to have bested her.

"Lady," the Elder of the fisher-people said, "what are you meaning to do?"

"I must seek him," she said. "I must get back what he took."

They made a sound; they had been hushed before.

"If you go, who will tend the shrine? There has always been a maiden."

"The Relics are older than any maiden who ever served there. The Relics are the purpose of the shrine; it was built to house them. Two remain. I will bind them with seals no thief can break. Then I will pursue the third."

They fidgeted, avoiding her eyes. Because they respected her office and her power, they did not argue, only asked questions.

"If you are gone, how shall we observe the Ritual?"

"I will speak the Ritual for you, as ever," she said, "at dawn and at sundown, without fail, as I travel, wherever I may be. I shan't forget. It will be the tie that links me to you. To maintain the shrine you should choose women by lots. They will sweep the floors and light the lamps, as I do. Whenever you go to pray or to offer, you keep the shrine holy. God will be near you, if you reach for him. You do not need a priestess so much as faith. Indifference kills faith, and lack of faith puts out the torch of God that burns in each of us. That is why I cannot be indifferent to the theft of the sacred thing."

"Lady, you may be long away."

She was aware the Elder implied that she might die, and never return.

She bowed her head. Their perplexity hung on her like a cloak.

"If I am long away," she said, "you will have to elect a new priestess from among you."

"But that is far from tradition. Each must be taught. Only you know the ancient language—how can she read the Book unless you teach her? She will not be able to recite the prayers."

"Then," said Oaive, "she must simply pray as her heart suggests to her."

They muttered sullenly. She was abandoning them. They did not understand her impulse, the importance of this deed to her. Naturally, they had never seen the Bone, experienced the quickening that seemed awake in it. But it was more than this. It was not merely what had been stolen . . . she could not really explain, even to herself, what impelled her to follow the thief. It was like breathing. She could do nothing else.

The faces of the women were like rock, except for one or two who wept. She took some of the older ones to her chamber by the shrine. She showed and explained the unguents and philters to them, and what they were to be used for. At first, the women seemed to be refusing to comprehend, out of resentfulness, but at last a widow in the group, used to fending for herself, became practical, began to answer yes or no, and to ask sensible questions.

When they had gone, Oaive put away the shells she had not painted. It was a fine white day; she did not need to light the hanging lamp, as she sat to tie off all the threads of her weaving. As she was doing this, suddenly she noticed that two had frayed and were broken. A fist seemed to clench on her heart. Was this also an omen? The broken thread, sign of severed ties, or of death itself? She recalled the words of the Elder. But she set her foreboding aside; there was no time for it.

An hour before sunset, she began her search for a clue.

She felt sure the violated shrine would have retained some evidence of his coming, his wolf's going, however slight, to help her. Even if it were only a hair from his sea-silver head.

She picked about the court as intently as a bird. She discovered nothing. Eventually she thought of the wall over which he had climbed.

She went outside the courtyard, and studied the rough surface of the wall. In the angle between two blocks, a tiny scrap of grey cloth was caught, torn off by the sharp teeth of the stone.

So I have you, she thought with grim triumph. Her heart beat fast, warming her. She was surprised by her determined hunger to catch and destroy him.

She said the sunset Ritual, on purpose, outside, standing on the steps facing the bay. The sky behind her was angry, and the sea darkening. She had a sense of insecurity and excitement, as if she might never see this spot again.

Afterwards, she went inside. She put the piece of material between her palms. She shut her eyes, and forced her mind into the fibers of the cloth.

It was difficult, then more difficult. She must hold the course of her brain as the fisher-people held the course of their boats. In the end her will pierced through as abruptly as a needle.

The cloth had been in the grey man's possession; ripped from him, it still belonged to him, still hankered for the garment of which it had been part.

The cloth had memorized the pulse of a wrist, an iron armlet, it came from the left sleeve of his tunic. . . . Now there was a slap of reins, a horse galloping in Oaive's mind, a rider bowed to meet the wind. Beyond the mist, across the hills, inland, where the rivers tipped over heights to rush and foam. Westwards.

Oaive withdrew her concentration. She could follow him from this moment on, the wolf-thief. The cloth would be her guide.

She felt tired. She lay down to sleep, ready clothed for her journey, her feet bound with strips of hide, over her knees the cloak of fleece the sheep-people had given her long ago.

She did not sleep at once; when she did, she had a dream. She dreamed a rope bound her to a post standing in the sea, and she cut the rope and walked away inland, into the glare of the furious falling sun.

It took her three days to cross the hills.

Southwards, the great woodlands spread blackly into a distance of softer blackness. Like the sea, once begun, the woods appeared to have no end. And north and west the surges of the hills, pocketed with caves and like the backs of half-bald pitted stony animals, seemed equally limitless.

She missed the sea almost at once. The sound and sight of it, its old drowned smell. She missed, too, the safe shrine, the familiar routine of her days. Here everything was unknown, even how she must deal with it. If she had had no purpose, she would have been terrified by her freedom.

She carried a little food in a bag at her waist, not much. She knew which plants to eat, and where they might be found; she did not want to be weighed down by provisions. He was a day and nearly two nights ahead of her. Nevertheless, she paused, dawn and sunset, to say the Ritual. The words were flimsy out here; they had lost their meaning away from the shrine.

None but the sheep-people dwelt in the hills, grazing their flocks on the thin grass. Men and beasts were small and woolly, and both had bleating voices. The shepherds greeted her formally; even so far from the coast they knew her as their priestess. After the second day, when she no longer met them, she began to lose the sense of who she was. Her own people were behind her now.

The thief had a horse; occasionally she noticed its droppings on the ground. He must have tethered it, while he was at the shrine, in a cave or one of the drystone bothies the shepherds used during lambing. The scrap of cloth was her guide. If she concentrated on it, she could feel the pulse in his wrist and glimpse the horse galloping. She would not lose him, but could she ever catch up?

Presumably he rested, the horse would need to rest. Sometimes she came across the ashes of a fire. At night, when she was too tired to go on, she lay down in her cloak under a bush or rock. She herself seldom made fire. Her feet were hard and strong, and she was also strong. She did not sleep more than three or four hours.

On the evening of the third day, she gazed from the last slope, and saw below her how the hills crumbled away into an ocean of wasteland, a wild heath. The long grasses tossed and rippled like the waves of the sea. The trees were gaunt, twisted and solitary. A white moon hung low, and the wind seemed to be blowing it by degrees off the edge of the sky.

The openness of the terrain disturbed her.

She crossed through grasses that stood as high as her ribs. The moon set, but the blackness was ferociously gemmed with stars.

In the morning, there was a village. She had slept within reach of it and not known, just over a rise in the land.

There were ten huts set among a winter-stripped dapple of fields, their roofs constructed of turf. Smoke rose thick as birds from the chimney-holes.

The one who called himself Grey had passed through this place, she could tell.

A track led into the village, creeping between the huts to a space of beaten earth where there was a well. Two women were already there, filling their household jars. They looked up and right at her.

"May I draw some water?" Oaive asked them. The women did not speak, but most villagers were odd at first towards strangers. She said again: "May I draw some water? I've come far and I'm very thirsty."

The two women did a peculiar thing. They moved back from the well and from her, still staring at her. One set down her jar carefully, the other held her jar too tight. Just at that moment a girl came from a doorway nearby. She took in everything immediately, and let out a high wordless screech.

Oaive began to be afraid. Shc calmed herself. In spite of them, she let down the bucket into the well and drew water, and drank from her cupped hands. While she was doing this, she was aware of the space filling with people, close-packed together because they kept such a lot of room between themselves and her.

Finally she looked up. There was a tall broad man a short distance from the front of the crowd. She spoke to him.

"My thanks for the sweet water."

His face was closed tight on itself, determined to give nothing away. He said, barely moving his lips: "You'll be going now."

"Yes, if you wish. Have you seen a man in grey, with grey hair?"

"You will be going now," the man repeated blankly.

"Answer my question first."

There came a seething from the crowd, like a pot on the boil. Suddenly something sharp struck her shoulder. Someone had thrown a flint.

"Stop!" The man shouted about him. "Are you all fools?" He squinted back at Oaive. "Yes. He has been here. And told us you would come after."

The water she had drunk was raw in her throat. She should have known, she thought, that the grey wolf would learn, by his own powers, that she followed him.

"Why are you afraid of me?" she asked the man.

A woman's voice yelled at the back of the mob: "Drive her out! Kill the witch—kill her!"

Oaive turned in the direction of the voice.

"If I am so terrible," she said, "how do you imagine you can kill me?"

She left the well, and walked exactly towards the crowd, which parted to let her through. She went up the track between the last huts. As she reached the outskirts of the village, a shower of small stones rattled behind her.

Clever Grey.

She could guess his story, and the way he told it.

The wicked witch from the coast pursued him, for the

sake of vengeance. Probably without cause. He had twisted the ears of her pet cat, or trodden on her toad. The witch was mad, evil, and had sly magics. Avoid and beware of her. She might only seem a young girl but that was just the guise she took on to fool you. Under it she was old and foul, with snakes for hair.... And when Oaive went back over his words to her, and his deeds, she wondered if he, too, believed some of his own tale.

She walked the rest of the day across the wasteland. There were no more villages. But the next day, at noon, she marked a huddle of dwellings, and skirted them. A man was out in the scrubby fields. When he saw her, he turned his face and strode off too fast.

She had meant to ask for food on her journey when her provisions were gone. Perhaps she could have performed some service in payment—healed a sickly child with her herb-lore, or cleaned pots if there were no other task. Now no one would give her food and no one would want her aid. Grey had seen to this. She had underestimated him, for all she had glimpsed of his skill.

She lived entirely off the land after that. She ate the sour roots that grew on the heath, and drank from the bitter streams. The waste was a cindery green, brown with autumn's burned-out gorses and wild iron-purple heathers. Often it rained, but never for very long. The cloak of fleece kept her warm and almost dry.

She said the Ritual dawn and sunset. Sometimes she forgot a word. It was as if the alien landscape had eaten it from her mind.

On the ninth day of her travelling, Oaive saw a ruined tower on a hill with a sprawling village wrapped round it.

There was a bell ringing; it had a dismal sound, like a burying. She had meant to keep clear of the houses, but there was a pool near the base of the hill, among some trees.

As she was drinking, she noticed a procession winding down from the village towards the pool. There were men in black robes she took to be priests. Their faces were rigid and pale, and they were shaking the wooden rattles the superstitious used to disperse demons.

On either side of the priests, and behind them, came men with a whole pack of dogs, restrained on short leashes.

All at once she realized it was not a procession.

She got up and went out of the trees, and paused on the other side of them. The villagers paused too. The priests pointed. One dog bayed and set off the other dogs. Their tongues hung from their mouths like tongues of flame. She knew these people were going to set the pack on her. They had kept the dogs mean and hungry—they would tear her in pieces. The bell went on ringing in somber pangs.

The men slipped the leashes. The dogs came springing down the slope like rocks, directly at her.

Oaive put her hands to her face. She wanted to scream, but she held herself firmly and compiled her strength. She shut her eyes and breathed deep. I cannot see you, therefore you cannot see me. You cannot scent me, you cannot sense me. I am a shadow of the tree. I am not here.

It was hard to hold the illusion together. The panting and howling of the dogs seemed likely to blow her magic from her like a fierce wind. The tide of them lapped round her. Their bodies thudded against her legs and they sniffed at her ankles. The need to open her eyes, to look, was overwhelming. Then the dogs were running on, past her, back the way she had come. They had not found her. The spell had worked.

She did not glance towards the people on the hill, who were shouting and cursing. As far as they were concerned, the witch had vanished into air. She knew if she looked at them, however, they would see her again, so she did not turn their way.

The tolling of the bell and the baying of the dogs stayed with her many miles across the waste, and that night she dreamed of them, and for several nights to come.

The land seemed to change in a night. She lay down to sleep on the heath, but the spoked wheel of the dawn sun showed her, on the horizon, a rocky, rising place, a place like the stairway of a giant's house. She had been weary and had not seen these rocks ahead, black on the black sky.

She said the Ritual, and went on, and an hour or so later she began to apprehend how high she must climb.

It was a merciless ascent. The wind beat her as she scrambled from one ledge to the next. Her whole body ached almost unbearably, but she seldom rested. Two hours after noon she reached the summit, and sat down there to get her breath and her bearings.

It was like being at the top of the world. The waste behind was a greenish shadow. Before, the rock cascaded into a plain dense with trees, where a huge distant stretch of water lay like a broken looking-glass, its surface scored bright as pitted silver. She thought for an instant she had come to the sea again, but then she took in its tideless, static quality. This was a lake. Miles off, other heights, like her own vantage point, stabbed over the lake. Here and there a thin white pillar joined rock-peak and water: a waterfall.

Oaive had never seen anything like this in her life. The wind was like a flashing blade; like old wine, it went to her head. Then she remembered her purpose for sitting there at all.

She stared across the wooded lake-plain. Nothing moving caught her eye, only a great winged bird stooping low above a cloud of pine.

Oaive took the piece of grey cloth from her belt, and held it between her palms. Presently she lifted her head, eyes wide. It was as though the spark in the cloth had died. Nothing came from it any more, no pulse, no picture, no guidance.

The great bird hung motionless, as if nailed to the air, then plummeted from sight.

She was a fool. If Grey knew she followed, he would guess her method in the end. So he had bought, bartered, or stolen a tunic from one of those villages he had warned against her. When he judged the moment ripe, he had exchanged the old garment for the new. The tunic, now that he no longer wore it, relinquished its borrowed sentience, and the link, cloth with cloth, snapped. She had lost him. Or had she?

Grey was there on the plain. Her instinct *told* her. It was the lake he was making for. He would need to cross it. And perhaps he was at ease, finally thinking her outwitted. . . .

She began the descent towards the trees, and her hands, rock-bruised already, started to bleed.

The sun had set by the time she reached the foot of the rocks. Pine trees and larch grew thickly under the slope, dividing the last burnish of the afterglow with their slanting shade.

She slept in the wood that night. It was mild, and small animals, not yet wintered-down, galloped about in the scanty undergrowth; a fox pattered by like rain over the carpet of fallen needles.

Before sun-up, she was pressing on with a determination to find Grey or his trail. How had he brought his horse across the rocks, or had he? She had noted none of its droppings this side of the height. She said the Ritual at dawn, but speaking as she walked.

A mist had come up like smoke, filling the wood. The trees were soon wrapped in it, their hard stems appearing to become transparent.

Abruptly, through the mist, she saw a man standing ahead of her in a clearing.

Oaive hesitated. He was facing her, tree-still, and he made no movement and no sign, even though he must see her now. Perhaps he was afraid of her, like the others. Perhaps he had a flint ready to throw, or worse, a spear or a knife.

She slowly raised her arm, to greet him, to discover how he would react. When he did nothing, she went forward again.

There was something peculiar about him, this man. Not merely how he waited there, motionless, silent. The shape of him was somehow wrong, his stance, the manner in which he held his arms so stiffly. . . .

Then suddenly she was close enough to glimpse what the figure really was. A scarecrow.

Two sticks for legs, fixed firmly into the earth, two awkward stick arms. The body was a sack of straw, tied tightly about three-quarters of the way up, to give the illusion of a head. In the villages by the sea, they made such things to keep birds from the crops. This one was a little different. A face had been daubed on it, two round black eyes and a grinning mouth. It had a cruel and acutely horrible look, laughing mercilessly at her there in the mist. Over its sack body and stick arms and the tops of its stick legs hung a single garment. A grey tunic with a torn left sleeve.

Yes, he had known. He had stolen the scarecrow from a field, clad it in his tunic, and left it for her like a message, a mockery, having painted the mockery on its scarecrow face.

The hair shivered on her neck. The scarecrow frightened her, and for a minute everything frightened her, what she had done, what she planned to do, the wood and the plain beyond, and the whole world outside the shrine.

But the mist was fading, taking doubt with it. She went by the scarecrow, and found herself in the outskirts of the pines. And saw what the pines had hidden from her.

The ground slanted downwards unexpectedly, clothed in muddy winter fields. At the bottom, about half a mile off, a shallow valley had been formed, which ended near the skyline where an arm of the lake reached back into the land. In the valley, a second wood, a vast forest of wooden dwellings and stone towers.

A ray of the early sun ignited the lake beyond. Ships lay out on the water, seeming tiny from here as scattered seeds, with gnat's-wing sails.

That was the way he had run, her enemy. She was certain. He had even taken time for his joke—the scarecrow thieved from their fields. No doubt he had sold the horse, here, or the other side of the rocks. He would have used the coins to buy passage on a ship; he would already be sailing for another shore. She sensed him gone, ahead of her yet.

But he was still the quarry, she the hunter.

Did he maybe think witches could not cross water?

3. Red Ship

"MY BROTHER," she said persistently, "are you certain you've not seen my brother? You cannot miss him, I'm sure. His hair is red as a carrot, and his shoulders—like so—one higher than the other. And he is freckled—"

"No," said the man impatiently, "I have not seen him."

"But I was told in the town that a man came and asked for passage on a ship. I was told. Wasn't he my carrot-haired brother? The wretch who left my father and me with the farm to manage alone through the winter—yes, and took our savings from the cracked pot under the hearth-stone. Oh, if I can but catch up with him! Didn't he come here seven days ago?"

"It was the day before yesterday the traveller came, and left yesterday eve," grumbled the man, anxious to be rid of this chattering nuisance of a farm wench, "and he was a rover, a man of breeding, with a sword at his side."

"And red-carrot hair?"

"No, no, by all the—*grey* his hair was, strange hair on a young man. And a wolf pelt on his back. Is that likely to be your brother, eh?"

"If you say you saw him—"

"I do say. It wasn't a humble passenger's place he wanted, either, but to hire a ship and pilot and crew to himself. Kurl's Red Ship it was. And there's Kurl's boy, Kurl. Go bother him, and leave me in peace."

Oaive had not known if Grey would have agitated the people here against her too. She thought not, for he would imagine he had left her behind; besides, it was not an isolated village, suspicious of any stranger. Rumor could not get such a hold here. This town traded with other towns across the lake, and the ships went back and forth from shore to shore, and some farther, out from the lake at its western end, where a wide river breached the stronghold of mountains.

Still, Oaive had risked no chance. She had gone straight to the harbor where a tall tower guarded the brink, and the vessels were massed like a swarm of bees on the water. There, opening her eyes wide as wide and hanging her mouth open as well, she managed to give an impression of being very young and rather stupid. She invented a story and made a lot of fuss. She knew the knack people had of answering the one question you did not ask. If she had demanded information concerning Grey, perversely, they might have refused her. But, through her pecking and jabbering round them like a hen after her make-believe brother, people were helping unintentionally in their efforts to be rid of her.

Kurl's boy, Kurl, was a scruffy, sullen lad tarring the keel of a boat in the shipyard by the harbor. He pulled at a thin whisker or two on his chin, as if encouraging them to grow.

"Yes, Old Kurl hired a man his Red Ship. Just the ten of them went out. Dog, Gil and six more for the oars and to crew her, Old Kurl as pilot and the grey man. She's but a small craft."

"Grey man?" Oaive whined. "My brother has—"

"Yes, girl. So I'm hearing. But this one is grey. It's the ship that's red."

She made an "O" of both her eyes.

"It's his whim," said the boy sourly. "My father, Old Kurl, he's a fool for wanting to be known. So he paints her red, and stains the sails red. And when anyone sees her they supposedly says: 'Aaah! There goes Kurl's Red Ship.'" He gave a sneer.

"My brother would go east," Oaive insisted stubbornly, "so the ship will go ea—"

"The ship won't. It's going west, to River's Mouth," cut in young Kurl triumphantly. "Thus you had better seek your kin elsewhere." And he turned back to his task.

Oaive snivelled briefly into her sleeve and went away.

There was a deal of the day still left. She could do nothing more till night came. She went up the street, into the busy market-place of the town. Here she picked out a good spot, not too far in, but near the well where the women would come. She sat cross-legged in her cloak. When a woman passed near enough, Oaive called in a soft compelling voice: "Let me tell your fortune, lady. Let me bring you luck."

Almost all the women she called looked about at her, and many stopped, most to haggle, trying to get something for nothing. A few pressed a brown coin into Oaive's palm, and let her scan theirs.

She read more by touch than by the roads of the hand, but she read truly. Occasionally she saw some bad thing, and then she advised them how to avert it. Generally their lives were to be uneventful, fruitless as dead trees, and then she embroidered her talk somewhat, to make them happy. It is not unpleasant to anticipate good. It hurts no one, and if the good never comes, you can still be hoping it will.

Late in the afternoon the air set cold and the clouds were large in the sky. Oaive took her coins to a line of baker's ovens and bought a loaf.

When the sun had fallen and the dusk pressed low on the streets, the men came from the harbor and into the houses or wine-shops. Oaive went back to the lake. A beacon was burning at the head of the stone guard-tower, and three or four men went about here and there to keep watch on the ships. She drew the shadows round her and walked soft. When a man was close, she shut her eyes and was invisible.

She chose a narrow boat in the dark the far side of the tower. Its sail was furled, but she did not immediately require its sail. She charmed the rope that bound it to the quay. She stepped into the boat, and the rope released the boat from the ring, and dropped on the deck.

Oaive spoke to the boat: "You need no oar, you need no sail, you need no wind to move you." She whispered old words, and the boat stirred under her like an animal in sleep. Presently it glided out on to the lake.

The water was smooth as ice. The yellow light from the tower floated on it. If anyone saw her, or saw the oarless boat flying so far without sail, they did not accept the evidence of their eyes, and remained quiet.

Oaive sat aft in the boat to steer.

A fish leaped in the lake like a dagger.

About midnight the clouds blew overhead. Oaive let out the sail and it bent like a bow. She tacked before the wind and the boat ran light as a deer. Oaive was of the fisher-people. She had learnt something of their way with boats before ever she visited the shrine.

She steered among a colonnade of waterfalls.

Later she secured the sail, and the tiller by the rope to her waist, the sailor's trick, so any sudden change of wind or the vessel's tempo should rouse her, and slept a few hours.

Grey was only a day ahead of her. He had idled, carelessly. Only one day ahead, in Kurl's Red Ship.

In the morning the land was a ruff of shadow to north and south. Behind and before was only white water under a white sun.

She ate a piece of bread. The lake-wind still carried her, she had no cause to use magic. What she had done already surprised her. The spells were all off-shoots of more ordinary ones concerning binding and unbinding, the art of Aura, and the influence an adept might gain over the perceptions of others. When she had been taught the beginnings of these sorceries, she had never thought she would use them quite as she had, possibly never thought to use them ever.

At noon the wind died again, and Oaive motivated the boat. It occurred to her then that she could catch up to the Red Ship, for, with the wind down, they had only oars. In the midst of the crew, Grey would not resort to a trick like hers unless he had discovered her pursuit.

She sat by the tiller, watching, waiting.

The day ran by like the water.

Just before sunset the westering solar disk was divided by a tall mast, its sail furled on the yard. As the outline of the whole vessel stole up into view, Oaive saw it was the Red Ship, becalmed on the copper surface of the sundown lake.

She did not alter pace, and gradually she made out figures. One stood aft, not the pilot. She knew it was Grey.

Something like a dart of pain went through her, head to feet. And in that moment she was aware he saw her too.

Oaive heard him shout, across the water between

them. He was not shouting at her but because of her. He raised his arms. Then the wind came.

It fisted the smaller boat like a blow. Oaive was flung sideways, snatching hold of the tiller. The sunset dazzled into premature blackness. The wind appeared to come in a huge funnelling like an enormous wheel bowling down the sky. She understood that he had called it, summoned this wind as a man whistles a hound.

The sail unfurled and cracked taut on the Red Ship's spar. The ship raced westwards, and the water plunged aside like scythed sheaves. The violent wake slammed Oaive's craft like a whip.

Her sense of spell-weaving left her. The wind drove her boat now. The wind broke the lashings of the sail, which fell free and flapping. She was afraid and angry, both at once. The boat dashed on.

Lake and sky were the color of lead. She could no longer distinguish the Red Ship; it had vanished in a whirling of wind and cloud. The water seemed to be boiling as if enormous creatures were struggling up from the depths of it.

A lightning slit the seams of the dark. For a split second Oaive glimpsed the ship like a black swan in flight, transfixed by the glare.

What power of magic he had, to wake this. The elements went mad, and he had done it.

It was as if a whale thrashed under the boat, wanting to rise.

Suddenly the whale did rise, a juddering of the lake's back that sent the boat spinning. Oaive clung to the tiller. Everything reared upwards and fell down, and the water poured in. The world seemed to be standing on end. The boat hit a vertical wall of liquid. With a tearing bang the sail parted from the yard, and the boom swung inwards. Almost delicately, the edge of it struck Oaive across the forehead.

The lightning burst inside her eyes. She felt the tumbling craft pitch her out, but only vaguely, as if it did not matter. The water was so cold that after an instant she no longer remembered where she was.

She was warm, gently floating down through black silence.

Fool. Stupid witch-fool. Someone cursed in her ear. *Don't drown, you damned and worthless girl.*

She tried to blot out this disturbing voice. The silence was more friendly.

Fool. Listen, fool. The Relic. The Bone. I stole it from you. Are you going to let me take it after all? Oh, it's easy to drown, easier than making the effort to beat me. But you're going to, by the blood and soul in your body, you are.

Somewhere she hurt. Her body hurt. Abruptly she was fighting, kicking. Her head broke the skin of the lake and her hands gripped and ripped at the air to hold her up. A tough gritty piece of the air snagged between her fingers. She clenched her arms around it. It was the broken yard of her boat. Splintered planks were strewn in every direction, bobbing aimlessly. Presently the water gushed out of her like a pain.

She was lying over the yard. The lake was calm enough that she could see reflected in it the clearing sky and the stars behind. The wind was finished. She had meant to send back the boat she had taken, to the town, but there was no hope of that now. The boat was finished too.

There was a path of light through which she was moving. She raised her head. A rope was tied to the yard, pulling it, and her with it. The rope went up and over the side of the Red Ship, near where the lantern burned. Two men were hauling her in like a fish.

"Well, lady," he said, standing over her. "Well, well."

The deckhouse was low, windowless and dark, set amidships. Its walls were painted red outside and in, and the floor where she sat was heaped with rugs of scarlet wool. The coals in the bolted-down iron fire-pan were also red, as if to match everything else.

She had lost her cloak in the water. One of Kurl's crew had brought her a rough blanket to dry herself. None of them had spoken, or looked at her.

At first she had been so exhausted, she had not cared about her capture. She was confused. Surely Grey must have intended her to capsize. Why then have her saved? Perhaps he did not want the responsibility for her death? He could have killed her in the shrine, and had not.

The hostile crew reminded her of the hostile villagers. This bewildered her further. Grey was the magician, they had seen it. How could they think *her* dangerous after he had called the storm-wind?

Eventually he came into the deckhouse.

She thought she should hate him, as before, but she felt no fury, none of her former hunger for reprisal. Instead, she had a most extraordinary sense of relief, because his face was familiar and unafraid.

"Well," she repeated, "what now?"

"What now indeed. Aren't you going to blast me with your magic? You note they did not tie you up. No rope, of course, could hold you."

"Why are they in fear of me? After what you did—"

He smiled. His wolf teeth fascinated her. "I told them *you* did it. You were an accomplished witch; you brought the storm. I only tried to avert it with my poor and evidently feeble spells. When you fell in the sea, you should have heard them cheer. I made them rope the yard and fish you up. I said a ducking in water washes the witch-skill out of a woman until next full moon, and it would be bad luck to let you drown. How about that for a clever story? They'd believe anything if you make it sound silly enough. Anyway, you did lose your magic in the lake, did you not? When the wind came, you panicked like a goose with the wolf after it."

"You choose your words aptly," she said, "Grey Wolf."

She had anticipated this title would bring his malice to the surface, but it did not. His eyes went suddenly pale and sightless, as if he felt the onset of an old sickness which he knew and dreaded.

She recalled the voice in her ear as she was drowning, the voice which had nagged her alive. Grey's voice.

Oaive began to talk slowly, feeling her path to each sentence: "You could have stolen the Relic without visiting the shrine beforehand—yet you came, and in your fashion you told me what you meant to do. You realized I must go after you. You put trouble in my road—but I overcame it. Perhaps you knew I could. When I lost you, there was still a kind of guidance, as if I were *meant* to find you. The tunic on the scarecrow was like a signpost. And you wasted time in the town when you could have moved swiftly. You hired the gaudiest ship . . . you summoned the storm and you could have been rid of me in it. Instead—"

"You should have mastered the storm," he said to her. Amazed, she watched his face grow bleak with anger. "You could have mastered it. The power's there in you, if only you had the brain to harness it."

"So you wished me to—*overcome* your magic? It was a test of me? You are disappointed that I failed. Why?"

He stared at her, long, and very intently. She could meet any pair of eyes, it was in her training. But his eyes were not easy to meet. She could not read them, and somehow they demanded to be read.

"I can't tell you," he said in the end. "Maybe you'll reason it for yourself. It's a strange game we're playing, you and I. Though there is a third player also. He doesn't know it yet."

She said hesitatingly: "You appear to want my help; I can see no other reason for your actions. But you are more powerful than I."

"Am I? What is power?" he said.

"A spell is power."

"Spells are words, and words are merely noises. The spell is the crucible in which the ore of the magic is formed. But the magician is the stuff of the ore. I imagine not all the priestesses of your shrine were as clever as you—or were they chosen in some special manner that determined who would possess power? Anyone can learn the chants and gestures of the occult art; they can get every syllable and wave of the arm exact, but if there's no magic in them, there will be no magic made. Otherwise this world would be crowded with wizards, would it not?"

"I was instructed in these things."

"You are the sorceress, not your instruction. Don't limit yourself. I judged a while since what you might be capable of. When I went to your shrine and I found you sitting at your loom, like any fisherman's house-proud daughter, I thought nothing more of you than another. But when you brought down the fire, your worth shone through you like the flame. Then I thought: Here is a witch with witch-hair like tawny pale metal, and she can wring water from stone and set hills jumping. You proved me right till the storm, Oaive."

He had never spoken her name before. He must have asked it of the fisher-people. It made a curious bond between them, she was not certain why it should. What he said of her magic frightened and excited her. Yet she seemed half to recognize the truth of it, dimly, like figures in fog.

She said: "Give me back the Bone you stole, the Relic. I promise I will try to help you."

"Ah, no," he said, "you miss the point. I must take the Bone, and you must track me. I am bound. It is the game I mentioned."

"This is foolish."

"The binding that was laid on me was far from that," he said, and his mouth was white.

"Am I to follow you blindly, as if we had never had this meeting?"

"Yes."

"If you tell me nothing," she said, "I can do nothing."

"I will tell you my name," he said softly. "Yes, even though you could use my name to harm me. I am called Grey by many, but by a very few I am called Cyrdin. I tell you partly for selfish ends. One day I may need you to call me by that name. Perhaps you will not. Who knows?"

"Cyrdin," she said. A welling of compassion thrust within her. "Grey Cyrdin."

"I was born grey-haired," he said. "They gathered from that portent I should be a great sage and sorcerer. This hair shaped my life, such as my life is."

A man pushed open the door of the deckhouse. It was the one the crew tagged Dog for his long pointer's nose. His coming changed the mood between them. Dog carried a jug and a loaf. He put them near the fire-pan, and went out, glancing neither at Oaive nor Grey.

"Tonight," Grey said to her, "eat and sleep here. Tomorrow we resume our roles of hunter and quarry. At dawn, Kurl will weigh anchor. You'd best be gone by then. I have a notion the crew plan to sell you as a slave in River's Mouth Town—that's if you show no symptoms of returning witchery. On the other hand, they may get scared and throw you overboard, despite my advice. Once ashore you should be safe enough. It's but half a day's trek to the river. After that, seek my trail on the mountain road."

"First, how shall I cross to the shore?"

He smiled at her. "Make magic," he said. She stared at him. "Truly. I am not joking with you. There are a thousand ways for an adept to get dry over water. I explained my faith in your ability. Are you going to give up, and let me steal the Bone?"

"If I am as powerful as you make me out, I could kill you here, and take the Bone immediately," she said with bitter emphasis.

"Do it," he said, "I dare you." And grinned and went out of the door.

Oaive reached for the jug the man had left her. She drank the sour wine. She felt betrayed, almost humiliated, because she had stopped hating Grey. But it was no good. She could not condemn or fight him anymore. She sensed him in the grip of a terror and tragedy worse than any she had experienced or observed. And he had trusted her with his true name, although, as a witch, she might turn it against him. What he had told her, what he said she must do made no logic. Yet she found herself willing to do it.

She bowed her head and began to concentrate in upon her own mind, searching.

In the half-light moments before dawn, she went like a shadow to the prow of the Red Ship. Kurl himself was aft, keeping watch by the wheel. The lake was glass.

Oaive let fall the rug she had taken from the deckhouse. It settled and spread like blood on the water. She had no spell; she leaned towards it. "Bear me up," she murmured. "Bear me up as if I were weightless."

Kurl heard the murmuring. He swivelled in her direction but could not make her out, for she had shut her eyes. Lids fast closed, she got over the rail and let herself down upon the rug. Her feet touched the wool. Her mouth was parched. She would not let herself think what she did. The rug would carry her. She had no weight.

The rug was not wet. It dipped a fraction, no more. She grasped her brain in a vice.

To the shore now. Swift as a gull!

The rug darted forward eagerly, taking her with it. She opened her eyes. Cold as ice, and sweating with a fear she dared not let herself feel. If she doubted, she would sink. It was that simple.

The rug danced, carrying her. The water shattered before them.

Behind her, Kurl bellowed. He had seen her. She had no time or emotion to spare for him.

The shore came closer, a pebbled shore, glittering as the sun rose and started to strike sparks on it. Oaive's desperation to reach it was like an iron plant growing in her spine. She ached with it. She pulled herself towards the shore by her will and her eyes.

Then the rug ran up on to the pebbles.

Oaive cried out. Strength deserted her, but the ground was firm and safe. She had succeeded, worked the magic without spells, by her will alone. As Grey had told her she could. She began to laugh. Half-turning, she saw the Red Ship aswarm with its crew.

The sail splayed to the wind, and it fled across the lake, away from her.

Oaive laughed, holding pebbles in her hand.

4. Land of White Swords

A WATERFALL CRASHED IN THE LAKE, its sound broadening and retreating on the wind. The town of River's Mouth stood nearby, exactly where the lake narrowed and the river began. There was a wall about the town and behind the town another wall, this one of low mountains. They tumbled up at the sky, and the river wound away into them, shining.

Oaive avoided the town. From the slope she had seen a scarlet sail among the shipping and Kurl and his men might have talked about witches. She did not blame them. What she had done alarmed her, too. She took the track that ran beyond the town, the beginning of the mountain road.

At the river-ford they were selling shaggy ponies for the uplands. Grey might have purchased one in order to keep ahead of her. She had given over puzzling about his motives. A new truth was fastening on her.

Circumstances had prevented her speaking the Ritual yesterday and today, but this was not what troubled her. She had *forgotten* she should speak it until long after the hour was past. She had told the Elders she would not forget. When the sun set this evening, behind the heights, she halted, and chanted the old words with extra care.

She knew in her heart the quest had altered for her. The shrine was fading from her mind like a lamp going out. Grey had become the quest, and the Relic of Bone merely a symbol. He was like a question she must answer. So much she understood, though she felt shamed by her unintentional faithlessness to her people.

She met a shepherd in the dusk driving his flock. With her last coin she bought from him ewe's milk, and bread. He was a big dark man, unlike the shepherd-folk of the shrine villages.

She slept on a mountain that night, and next day walked over others. She was now used to seeing and doing things that were strange to her. Strangeness itself was becoming usual.

The road terminated abruptly on the second day, at a tiny crow's nest of a town, perched against the sheer wall of a crag. The crag seemed to be the last of all the heights, large enough to block out anything beyond it.

In the winding street, a woman said to Oaive: "I never before saw hair your color. You must be the one."

"Which one is that?"

"The one the grey man told me to spy out for."

This was new. Despite their conversation on the ship, Oaive had been half-expecting fresh obstacles and tests left in her path.

"Maybe I am she. What then?"

"Not much." The woman laughed, pleased with her errand and the importance of it. She led Oaive into a stooping house, and gave her a thick cloak of woven stuff and a packet of food. "He says you will need these," said the woman, for Oaive was staring. "He says go through the Rock Gate and take the pony-track down. And then, he says, guess the route as you did before." The woman's eye corners crinkled. "Odd goings-on, I must remark."

"Where is the Rock Gate?" Oaive asked.

"I will take you, if you will tell my hand."

"Did he say I would do that?"

"He said you are a witch," said the woman, "but I'm thinking he's fond. What witch would go footsore as you do, when she might fly?"

"What witch indeed," said Oaive.

She read the woman's palm swiftly. She was to have luck, which cheered them both.

This was an icy day. Oaive put on the cloak Grey had bought or stolen for her, and was glad of it. The woman conducted her through the town. At the back of the highest street stood the wall of the crag. When they were close, Oaive saw a stairway and, at the bottom, an arch-mouth cut in the rock face.

"Here's the gate. This is the way he went. Not many come or go through this door."

Oaive touched the woman's shoulder, and stepped under the arch. It was a passage, black-chill but not long, which wormed through the mountain. She looked back once, and the woman was waving from the entrance. The omens were not good—the dark tunnel, the signal of farewell. . . . Then Oaive came to the rock's other mouth, and paused.

The world had altered. She was in another country.

The crag descended to the floor of the plain below in terraces. The plain itself was slate-blue with shadow and distance. Far to the north a lost curl of the river was gleaming. Otherwise the view looked empty, clear to the horizon. There were new mountains there, not like these she had already travelled. They were slender and pointed. They stood in a rank like teeth set in the jaw of the land. She realized they must be immensely high, for their heads flashed burning white with snow. Oaive studied them, recognizing their shape as if she gazed on her own birthplace, rather than Grey's.

More than teeth, they resembled swords, dipped in white blood, balanced on their hilts against the sky. . . .

The plain was barren and bitter cold. When the sun set, the sword mountains turned black and terrible against its redness.

Five days she was on the plain, for weather and terrain made things harsh for her, and difficult. She met neither animals nor men. Sometimes she passed a ruin. Trees grew here and there, marking brackish watercourses. Maybe in spring the landscape would wake, but she did not think so. It was as though a plague had passed over it, killing everything, and then even the plague had died.

Thin snow sprinkled down. At night she created fire. The light and crackle of the flames seemed to echo all over the desolation. She considered the woman's words, how, she had said, a witch would fly. Oaive wondered dazedly if she could. Grey would tell her she could.

She reached the mountains on the sixth day.

They did not look real. They shimmered like effigies of polished marble. The plain meandered in valleys around and between them. She found a sort of road of cracked stone, and hail began to smash on it.

When the hail slackened, she stared up and saw that the road ended half a mile away, because a mountain had fallen in its path. This had occurred perhaps a thousand years before. A massive jumble of blocks, its highest tips were still blanched with snow; forest had fastened on its rifts like ivy on a collapsed building. The other mountains stood aloof, ignoring it. Their time, no doubt, would also come.

The forest called Oaive, but its voice was a wail of pain. She wanted to run away, it was so strong, this impression of distress.

She went on, towards the first swathe of trees.

Oaive dreamed she was a bird. She was flying over the fallen mountain. It was huge, the mountain. It stretched for miles, and between its bones and away and away to the west beyond it ran the evergreen forest.

Even the river came back from the north to forge a channel southwards through the trees below the mountain. The course was narrow here, but on its banks were the ruins of many villages. Young pines pushed through their walls. Oaive flew in at broken window-shutters, and out, as the wind did.

At sunrise, in the dream, she came on a towered stone house, standing on the eastern side of the river nearest the mountain. Inside the courtyard was a choked well. The wind had scoured through the open door, and left cones and twigs on the floor of a great lightless hall. The vast hearth was empty. A wide stairway led to upper rooms. In one of them a four-footed beast resolved itself from the cobwebs into a bed with a frame of carved pinewood.

Oaive perched on a post of the bed. A ray like sunshine sprang across the chamber. For a second she saw a little boy, not more than three years old, running and laughing there in some private child's game. His hair shone like pale iron.

Then she heard wolves.

They were all about her—in the house.

Their voices were composed of sadness and evil.

Oaive opened her eyes and sat up. She had been asleep beneath the trees, but now the sun was gliding above the forest. There were no wolves, no sound but the rushing of boughs.

* * *

The old man came unexpectedly towards her out of the forest. He was stooping awkwardly, picking up sticks and adding them to a bundle on his back. When he glimpsed her, he looked terrified, and when she spoke he turned and groped away.

After that, Oaive began to feel the forest was watching her, that hidden people observed her with morbid dislike. At noon she passed through a clearing. Three well-kept huts stood there, but the doors were fast shut and there were no signs of life, despite the smoke leaving their chimneys. She sensed ears straining and hands at mouths, and went on.

She made towards the river she had seen when she slept. She believed the dream had been true in some oblique fashion, and so was not surprised when she caught the glint of water below.

The sun was low when she reached the river's edge. It was as she had foreseen it, the channel matted with weeds, the ruins decaying on its banks. She felt a compulsion to seek the stone house. She did not want to meet the dusk in the open.

She found the house between one step and the next. The round moon was rising among its towers. This was Grey's home; he had been born under its gaunt roof to the sigh of the pines, as she had been born to the sighing of sea tides.

The door hung on its hinges. The floor was littered with twigs, as in the dream. Everything was like the dream, the hearth, the stairs, the shadows.

Oaive shivered. The house did not frighten her, but she felt an anguish in it.

She pushed closed the door, and spoke words to bind it closed. She spoke a word to the hall, telling its ghosts:

Be still. Gathering twigs from the floor, she set them on the hearth, and called fire out of herself.

It was hard to do, as if her magic did not want to help her in this place. The glow sped down her arm, at last, and burst upon the wood.

The flames filled the room with sudden brilliance, and she saw then the man who sat on the far side of the hearth from her, where the darkness had been before.

Her heart hit her breastbone. She kept perfectly still and made herself stare right at him, and she feared him at once.

The face of the man was very long and white. It was like the faces of the sword mountains; even the features, though curiously elongated, were almost flat, like an unfinished carving. He was heavily cloaked and hooded. The hood cast a shade over his unprominent brows, but she could see the eyes. They were impossible to describe. They were the colour of malevolence.

His mouth was virtually lipless, a slash. It opened, and he said: "You shall call me by the name of Niwus. You will need to name me. We are to have dealings together."

Oaive continued staring into his eyes. She gathered herself. "You tell me a name," she said. Her tone was steady and cool as she had made it be. "You tell me nothing else."

"I tell you much. You read my person. What do you read in me?"

"Great power," she said. It would have been stupid to deny it.

"You are right. *Great* power. What else?"

"You would have me presume," she said.

"The sea witch is exact. Sharp eye and sharp brain the eye serves. We are both priests. My shrine is here, some way up the fallen mountain, close to the sky, Oaive."

"I respect your wisdom, priest-lord. You know my name and where I come from; you knew that I would enter this house. Accept my homage."

"I will accept it, when it is truly given. I gained this knowledge not from my powers, but from my servant. I hazard you think I speak of a familiar or demon. No, Oaive. I speak of the grey man who stole the Relic from your shrine. For you see, he thieved the Bone for me, for White Niwus the priest. His Master."

Her mind ebbed to a sort of numb darkness. She remembered the boy from the fisher-village informing her excitedly: ". . . the stranger laughed—he said it was his penance to travel in winter—a priest laid it on him . . ." and she remembered too how Grey had murmured: ". . . there is a third player also."

"Does this surprise you?" Niwus asked her. His voice smiled; he did not. He would never smile. "Yes. It was my word he acted on. At all times. I foresaw that you would pursue the Relic, yet I told him he must provoke and anger you, put trials and barriers in your way. You would never have consented to journey here willingly. But you were proud, Oaive, jealous of your charge. You must pit your wits against the impudent stranger. You must hunt him down and vanquish him. Grey has been an excellent quarry, has kept your interest in the chase until the very end. And now you look into the snare, and you find a different animal from the one you sought."

"He gave you the Bone," Oaive said. "I am not necessary to your scheme."

"Wrong. You were the guardian of your shrine and the things of the shrine. This gives you an uncanny sympathy with the Bone—a link—which obviously you do not properly appreciate. I might acquire this sympathy, but it would take time, and I have wasted too much time already. You do not even understand the nature of the Bone, do you? Or my need of it?"

She thought of what Grey had said to her, that power came from within the magician himself, not really from ritual or spell or object. She wondered if Niwus had been told of their meeting on the Red Ship. Grey himself had seemed a mighty worker of magic. It came to her abruptly that the sorcery had not been his, but the loan of Niwus, intended to aid Grey on his master's business.

"Where is Grey?" Oaive said.

"He will be here directly. I have summoned him in a manner he recognizes. This was his home once. He was born here. This hall was very different then. There were tapestries and lamps. His mother worked colored thread at a great loom with silver lion's feet, and the black and red hounds of Grey's father lay before the hearth, growling over their meaty scraps. That family ruled all the region in those days. When Grey was birthed, he was heir to chests of bright coin and miles of rich land. And the priest lived humbly upon the mountain. It is a strange story that altered things."

Despite the binding spell she had set upon it, the door cracked suddenly open. Grey stood there, his wolf-skin cloak folded about him. His face was like a stone. He did not look at her, but came up the hall to Niwus.

Oaive said gently: "Tell me the story now, if you will, priest-lord."

"Yes. Maybe I shall. Or better, Grey here shall tell you."

Grey's eyes were fixed intently on nothing.

"What shall I tell the witch, my master?"

"Tell her the story of the nobleman's small son and the poor priest on the rock."

Grey began to speak, casually and lightly.

"When the nobleman's son was born with grey hair, they thought it was a sign on him of occult gifts. Actually, this was not so much the nobleman's belief as the conviction of the villages along the river which gave him fealty. However, Grey's mother heard the talk, and she too became convinced. She persuaded her husband that they should send the boy for instruction to the hermit-priest on the mountain. He was a devout man, this priest, and skilled in magic. But one winter he grew sick, and on a particular night he died. And this was how the nobleman's son—the boy I am calling 'Grey'—found him in the morning; bolt upright in his chair, and cold dead."

Grey paused. "Here is the amusing part of the story, isn't it, my master?" he asked, but Niwus never stirred. "Grey was thirteen years old, and he was afraid when he discovered the priest. He comprehended his tutor was dead, but he wildly dreamed that perhaps he could restore him. As a healer, the priest had access to a number of spells of cadamancy, the art which has to do with death. The boy had seen the tablets on which they were written, though the priest had forbidden him even to touch the box where they were locked. Now, in his grief, the boy smashed open the box and took out the tablets, and worked the spell; his sorrow and fear gave him the strength to call the magic. But the thing he drew was not the soul of the priest, which had already travelled too far to return. The conjuration attracted instead a wanderer, one of those spirits whose attachment to this world makes them chary of the next. Not all of them are evil, but many are. This one was old; it had wandered a great while and forgotten its past. Yet instinctively it seized the chance to live again in flesh. The spirit entered the body of the priest and, in doing so, absorbed the knowledge and the sorcerous science the priest had stored in his brain. When the boy saw flickerings of consciousness in the eyes and limbs of his tutor, he rejoiced. Then he found out his mistake. The rest of the story is very simple. The name of the spirit, or at least the name it manufactured for itself, was Niwus, and by that name it bound me. This was done in a moment. The priest had possessed understanding of sorceries he never used, being a good man, but Niwus did not reject these branches of learning. For six years since, I have served him. During those years the appearance of the priest's body has changed greatly. You will note, he resembles something unfinished, or bloodless. This is a reflection of his nature. Oh, Niwus doesn't mind how I insult him. He admits I have reason."

Niwus spoke. "You have not told her of your father."

"Ah. My father. I guessed we should come to that. Yes. He set himself against the magician, to get me free. It was a hopeless battle, and he lost it."

"Rather more," said Niwus quietly.

"Rather more? Very well. Oaive has seen what shape I become, she imagined, at my own will." Grey glanced at her for the first and only time, then away. "The snow was down, I remember, and Niwus stood in the snow outside this house, and he whistled me and I must come like his dog. I was sixteen. It was a feast day, and there were many in the hall, and the villagers had bonfires burning by the river, glittering in the water. My father came to the doorway, and he called his men to him, and the men of the villages too. He defied Niwus. He shouted to God to defend him, and drew his sword. Then Niwus said words. You could see them as he spoke them. They showed like mist on the air, and after that they faded. And as they faded, the spell in them took hold.

"My father sank on his knees. His mouth slavered, his hair grew down his back and over his arms. In the hall my mother screamed, but her scream was altered halfway. My father's hunting dogs were round the hearth. All at once they began to yelp and howl, and the whole mass of them burst out of the door and fled. Not a man or a woman of my family, not a man who stood beside my father, did the spell miss. Niwus had cursed us into wolves, Oaive, and wolves we remain. We *are* wolves. Except for Grey. The magician sometimes changes him to a man. But when Grey is wolf, his brain is nearly a wolf's brain."

Again Grey stopped.

Again Niwus spoke. "Tell her about the black wolf."

"Yes," Grey said, "the black wolf-skin I wear. It's a sort of joke of my master's that I should. I killed the black wolf, not with knife or bow, but by sinking my teeth in his throat when I was as he was. He was the leader of the pack. Wolves will fight for pack leadership. Now I am leader."

"Who?" said Niwus. "Who was the black wolf that you killed, whose pelt you wear as my joke?"

Grey's eyes were white with the tide of fury and pain so hardly held back. His voice was noncommittal.

"My father was the black wolf. I killed my father."

Oaive held her breath. The air seemed thick with poison. She looked at Grey, then she looked at Niwus. Niwus murmured something. The word seemed to hurt her ears, even her mind. She closed her eyes, and when she opened them again, Grey was gone.

At the edge of the firelight a grey wolf half-stood, half-cringed. Its irises were slots of silver. It snarled deep in its chest, watching the magician.

"Go, wolf," said Niwus, "go bawl at the moon."

And the wolf flung round, and ran from the hall into the night.

5. Black Room, Black Road

OAIVE SAT IN THE DARK. She was trying to think what she should do.

With her eyes shut, it was easy to pretend she was back in the shrine by the sea, and the noise of the forest was the sound of the waves. For a moment she let herself pretend this. But it was no use. It was no answer.

Niwus had been gone three or four hours. He had told her that in the morning, at dawn, she would come after him to the top of the fallen mountain. That was where the hermit-priest's dwelling was. That was where Niwus would work magic with the Bone, and she would help him. She did not want to help, to participate in his game of cold sorceries, but she knew he could make her do so. His power was everywhere, like the smell of the winter itself. She had dared use none of her own abilities in his presence. She had not argued or spoken at all.

She thought of Grey. Of wolves.

She must not think of these things. She must think of a plan. She stared into the burned-out hearth.

* * *

The sun woke her. Its light edged under the lopsided door. She had been dozing. She had not thought of a plan.

Then she felt it. It was like a rope tied about her, tugging.

Niwus was calling her.

She thought: He *needs* me for this spell. I am important.

Outside, she paused long enough to say the Ritual before starting her climb.

The land shelved up steeply from the river-bank. It had taken her almost all day yesterday to cross the mountain's shanks and reach the river, but here there were ancient trackways that enabled her to move quickly.

Just before noon the trees began to thin, and she could see great distances again, across the forest to the lower valleys and their stalagmite peaks. Then she saw a building outlined above her on the flashing air. Compact and dark, it suggested to her an animal crouching to spring, but when she got closer, she found how dilapidated it was. Part of the outer wall of the hermitage was down, and wild plants sprawled on the stone. It stood out on an empty treeless plateau. The sky looked near as a roof.

Oaive went to the arch in the ruined wall, through the courtyard, and came to the main chamber, a hall one story high. Inside the doorless doorway she could discern only blackness. It was like the shrine. She wished she were back there.

"Niwus," she said, "I am here."

Someone spoke to her out of the blackness. "Enter then."

She could see no alternative. She obeyed.

It was pitch-dark, despite the opening behind her. After a moment she made out another door ahead. The lintel and the upright of the door glowed very faintly.

"Walk this way," the voice said. It was Niwus' voice, unembodied, floating in space.

When she passed through the door, she was in a room that appeared to be much larger than any room in the hermitage could possibly be. The high domed ceiling was pierced by small slits of windows that she had not seen from outside. A cool unnatural daylight shafted down from them into the area beneath. Each of the shafts was distinct from the rest, and they crossed each other like broad silver threads, with the gloom between still thick as wool.

At the room's center stood an altar of granite. Beyond it, in the beam of one of the light shafts, Niwus was sitting in a tall-backed chair.

"Oaive," he said immediately, "call fire to the altar."

She took a step before she meant to. She stopped herself.

"If I am to assist your magic, tell me what it is to be, so I can do my part properly."

He said nothing. He held up a hand of pale twig-like fingers. On the smallest finger was a ring of yellow gold. He had the Relic, the tiny narrow bit of Bone. He was rolling it like a plaything, back and forth, between thumb and forefinger.

"Here it is," he said. "It's very powerful. I don't know why. Perhaps it is only because generations of priestesses have venerated it, and built up its power. You venerate it, do you not?"

Oaive had caught back a cry. For it was more than veneration. It was like regaining her lost child, or a treasure from the sea.

"From the beginning of this second life of mine," he said, "I have sought the Bone and its magic. I do not recall what life I lived before this. I lost my memories when I lost my flesh. Now, I daily forget the memories of my spirit-existence since I have flesh again. Yet, from the very first, it always seems to me, I sought the Bone and its magic. I knew it. It is a sort of dread, and a sort of yearning. Presently and together we will bind it with spells. Then I shall grind it in powder. I shall eat it; its sorcery will pass into my blood, become part of me. I shall not have to fear or seek it any more. Its magic will be mine."

"No," she said.

He looked at her. "No?" he asked. *"No?"*

She trembled, barely knew what she was saying. It was idiocy to defy him, yet she did it.

"No, I will not help you."

"I will make you help."

"You cannot," she said. "You dare not harm me, you need my assistance. If I refuse, you can do nothing."

"I can punish you," he said. "I can cause you to wish you had not invited my impatience."

She felt her rebellion like rock inside her.

"Do that," she said.

There was a shift in his eyes as if a worm had twisted through the sockets behind them. Then he blinked out like a candle flame.

The light of the high windows died. It was blind black; she could see nothing. She circled involuntarily about and her hand slapped on stone. She groped along it. She went on and on. There was no longer any break in the wall that she could find, no way out.

He was gone, and he had trapped her in the belly of the hermitage, if this really were the building she had seen at all.... The black pressed between her lids like fingers trying to thrust her eyes more deeply into her head.

She lost her balance abruptly. In the dark she could scarcely tell up from down. She made herself sit on the cold floor. She quietened herself. She spoke spells of unbinding. They did no good. Of course, the prison might be entirely an illusion.

She leaned back on the wall, and tried to call fire from herself, to give her light. It would not come. The magic he had worked here was too great. What spell was left her?

Spells are words, and words are merely noises. You are the sorceress, not your instruction. Don't limit yourself.

But, Grey, I cannot even call fire.

Despair clawed up inside her. She began to weep. She had not shed tears since she was a child.

A man was walking over the snow. His feet and his long cloak made blue runnels in its whiteness. There was no sound in the forest. Then sound began to come in snatches from one direction only.

Emerging from the trees behind the man, she located the sound. Bonfires were leaping all along the river bank, reflecting in the water. There was music, pipes and stamping, the chink of bells.

Above, on the slope, the towered stone house, the snow trampled into slush about it by countless feet. Torches blazed in the courtyard, and the open door of the hall exhaled light.

The man whistled. She knew he did, though she did not hear him. He stopped still about twenty paces from the wall.

Grey came from the entrance in the wall. He was younger and very pale. He nodded to the man in the snow, and began to walk towards him. Then there was shouting. The sound of pipes and dancing ended. Somebody strode out after Grey. This man was tall, twice Grey's age, with coal-black hair. A sword pointed from his hip. He shouted and men ran to him, from the house, from the villages below, burning branches in their hands, knives, staves and stones.

"This is the end of it," Grey's father said. "You will grant my family peace."

The man in the snow did not reply.

Grey said: "Father, let it alone, let me go with him."

"Be silent. You have done enough. Now I will undo it. God is my defense." He called out to the sky, and the sword grated from its scabbard.

Then Niwus spoke.

"You howl like a wolf, and the pack bay at your heels. You shall be what you seem."

Oaive struggled to wake, to leave the dream. She did not want to see. But she saw it all. The words on the air like smoke, the men falling to their knees, and the change which remade them. She heard the women scream, and their voices break midway into beasts' wailing. She saw the hounds run out of the hall with their eyes starting from their heads.

After that she woke up, but it was not like waking. She felt as if her soul fell back into her, as if it had gone travelling. She remembered then the other dream, how she had seen the house, and Grey as a child, playing there. . . .

There was a gleam in the blackness. She flinched from it. Little whirling specks of brilliance came together and formed Niwus, or his shape, at the other end of the room.

"I have returned for your answer," he said.

She did not know how long she had been here; it seemed to have been days, but her mood had altered. Her tears and her dreams had honed her mind in a fashion she did not properly undcrstand.

"You shall have my answer," she said wearily. "I am sick of the dark. Let me free, and I will do whatever you want."

"Excellent," he said.

He spoke a word to the shadows. They folded like cloth and packed themselves away.

She saw the hermitage as it truly was, at last. Dusk shone dully through the broken roof on the weeds and cracked walls. He stood by the altar.

"Come here," he said. "Call fire as I asked you before."

She walked slowly to the altar, moving dejectedly. She called fire. It was easy, now he was allowing her to practice her magic. The flames whirled on the stone. She accepted the fact that when she had helped him create the spell, her usefulness would be done. He would probably kill her.

The Bone lay on his palm. He offered it to her. "Take that, and consider what it was to you—that is how the sympathy is established between it and you. Then say what I tell you to say."

She hung her head as she took the Bone. But when her fingers closed around it a ragged surf of joy and confidence dashed over her, and almost made her betray herself.

Standing there, as if utterly wretched, she began to put on her Aura, and assumed it suddenly. The unseen glory sprang up about her, she felt weightless, towering. Then she stared at him.

Niwus' face was expressionless. She had never noted an expression on his face.

"Why do you do that?" he asked. He did not trust her, but neither did he fear her. She had surprised him when he thought her tame.

The Aura was at its peak. She raised her arm and cast down it the bolt of energy the Aura could be formed into. The light and the strength went from her, stunning and shocking her. She saw it explode from the fist with the Bone locked in it.

There was a flash like lightning. Niwus reeled aside. He made no noise, but she knew the charge had struck him, and he had had no shield.

Now there were only minutes—or seconds, for he was horrifyingly powerful—in which to escape, evade pursuit, hide herself.

She was recovering from the blow she had dealt. She fled by the altar, through two doorways, and came out on to the bare plateau.

She ran and scrambled towards the first trees. Branches whipped at her, but she snatched them to aid her progress down. Once she skidded and fell, but she never let go of the Bone in her fist.

When she had to pause for breath, she glanced back. Through the trees she could still just see the crown of the hermitage against the pallid darkness of the sky. Nothing moved on the plateau. Yet.

When she could neither run nor walk any farther, she chose the only refuge she could. She climbed a quarter of the length up the gnarled pillar of a cedar. Its boughs were broad as beams, and broader. She rested between them, the layers of foliage angling away below her. It was not safe here, but safer than on the ground.

The forest had seemed to have no end. She could not find a way out of it. Sometimes she had glimpsed the river, but never come to it. Even allowing for her agitation and the overcast, moonless night, she suspected a web of sorcery trapped her on the mountain. She had been aware of no pursuit, which troubled rather than reassured her.

Exhausted, she laid her head on the mast of the tree. She did not mean to sleep, but she slept at once.

The cold woke her.

When she opened her eyes, the tree appeared to be

soaring upwards through a maelstrom of white ribbons. In the end she grasped that it was not the tree which was flying, but snow coming down.

She pulled her cloak over her head, and curled herself into it. It had been snowing a long while before it roused her, the blackness of the tree was already heavily patched with white.

Finally, the snow stopped. Beyond and beneath the cedar the forest was quite different. The trees were like menacing white animals with shaggy coats and no faces.

Shadows flicked between the trees. To begin with, it might only have been the sheer whiteness bothering her sight. However, when the shadows thickened and drew closer, she could no longer believe that. A somber river was tumbling down through the forest towards her. It made no sound, but it had eyes. Wolves.

They loped all together, not hurrying, but steady, darting in and out of the trunks. There were many of them; she could not judge how many. They had been men once, and women, but now they had forgotten. They were only wolves. Niwus' wolves, his slaves and subjects. Niwus had sent them to track her.

The tide of wolves came in over the snow, and burst around the cedar.

They might have been all the same wolf, each silent, each staring up at her. When she looked straight down through the boughs, burnished eyes shone from between the roots of the tree.

If she shut her own eyes, would the spell of invisibility work? She shut her eyes, but she could trace no power in herself. She was too tired, too afraid. Grey had been right, then. It was not the spell but the vitality of the sorceress that mattered.

The wolves were pawing at the foot of the cedar. They began to whine and grunt to each other. Farther off, one let out a full-throated iron howling. The howl smote inside Oaive's head and her hair rose. Other wolves began to howl. The howls blended in different metallic colors.

Suddenly there was a disturbance right through the middle of the pack. A tall cloaked man was parting them like grass. Niwus. They leapt aside from him, biting and fighting their neighbors out of their way. He moved to where she could see him.

"While you were useful, you might have lived, witch. Now I cannot trust you, you will not live. I shall call you down. You will not resist. You will give me back the Bone. Then I will give you to them, my servants under the tree."

She had put the Bone in her belt when she climbed the cedar. She took it and gripped it in her hand. She knew a fear worse than any she had ever known.

How could she build a barrier against the magician?

She squeezed her eyes shut again. She held the Bone against her face. She thought of the shrine by the sea.

She could hear Niwus speaking the words to force her down from the tree. If she listened she would have to obey him. She must not listen to Niwus, but to the boughs which hummed in the wind like waves. Yes, it was working. The shrine was her home where she had grown and learned. She was sliding away from Niwus, deep into her own mind, towards the shrine, the House of the Bone. . . .

Yes. This was clever.

She could not hear Niwus anymore.

She could hear instead a priestess, speaking the Ritual in the shrine. It began with one voice, but shortly there were countless voices. She was hearing all the priestesses who had ever served the shrine. She was reaching back, back into the past of the shrine, back to its beginning, to the Relics themselves, which were the source of the shrine's holiness.

A Ring, a Stone,
A Finger-Bone—

Abruptly, she was no longer in the cedar. She was running on a black road in a black mist, and something hopped before her—the Bone.

She had let it fall and it had taken on life. It was leading her towards a place she could not see in the dark. The prayers of the priestesses had faded, or rather become part of the sea-murmur beyond the mist. *Beyond the mist*—even as she raced on, the phrase struck her. It was the expression the villages on the coast had used, when they meant the unknown terrain that strangers came from. How curious to think of that now. . . .

The sensation of ground under her feet ended. She was falling. Then the mist tore open, and she dropped through it, out of night into the harsh brilliance of a winter dawn.

Oaive knew where she was, and how she came there. She had travelled in time. And in place.

In desperation, she had dared match her own power against Niwus, and that power had pushed her across geography and across centuries, to the one sanctuary that might protect her and strengthen her—the site of the shrine. This was the era of the making—or discovery—of the Relics. They were the source of the shrine's magic as the shrine was the source of her magic. She had not planned, but instinctively she had catapulted herself into this earlier world to seek them and to seek their history, as a weapon against the magician.

Of course, she had travelled in time before. They were not after all dreams, when she had seen Grey as a child, or the casting of Niwus' curse. Now, however, she had not journeyed alone in mind, or spirit—which had given her the illusion of dream—but in flesh. She was *physically* present.

Oaive opened her fist. The Bone was gone. She had guessed it must be. It was only another proof that she should seek it again here. The Bone had led her here. It was her magnet.

She did not feel any panic or bewilderment. She did not ask herself if, having entered the past, she could return to her present. This was because she had experienced, for the first time and to the full, the might of her own sorcery. She marvelled. Grey had told her: if she would believe in herself, she could do all she must.

Presently she looked about. In the east, the sea rolled at ebb-tide. The bay was shallower than she remembered it. Behind, the spine of the western hills was sharper and more cruel than it would come to be, licked smooth by centuries of rain and sun. There was no shrine; they would build that later. There was an altar, though: a rough stone black with fire, jutting up from the headland.

On the mud flats below the cliff a few men and women were walking, looking for edible shipwrecks, crabs, or mussels. Sometimes they would dig in the mud with knives of dark red metal.

The sun stood the width of two hands above the water. Oaive turned and went to the altar. She began to say the Ritual.

Gradually she became aware of people coming up the cliff path from the beach, and along the brow of the cliff itself. They stopped when they saw her, dead still. None of them talked. Oaive finished the prayer. She called fire. It scalded down her arm, and when the arm glowed, showing its bones, the crowd whispered round her. Flame bloomed on the altar.

Oaive looked at the people.

Their faces were blocky, primitive, full of admiration

and fear. But it was not the kind of blind fear that made them run away.

She smiled at them, experimentally, and they showed their teeth back at her.

One of the men came up and spoke to her. He was not as tall as Oaive. The words he uttered were in a language she could grasp; it was like her own, yet bizarre, and with a different accent. She made out that he was the son of the Elder. He was asking her to come with them to their village. Obviously, they recognized and revered magic. He was saying: Could she heal a sick child?

She answered very slowly, looking at him to see if he understood. She would do whatever she could to help them. The man nodded vigorously. Certain gestures—smiles, nods—had remained the same then.

They began to go back along the cliff top, urging her to follow them with movements of their heads and hands.

6. Blue Cave

THEIR VILLAGE OCCUPIED THE AREA where the village of the fisher-people would be. But it was not like the fisher-village. The ground was marshy where it drew off from the sea, and everything was built up on short wooden legs to keep it clear of the wet. The dwellings were huts constructed of mud, with a hole rather than a chimney to let out smoke. There was no long-hall, and the Elder's house was hardly bigger than any of the others.

The Elder's teeth were black with age; his mind seemed to wander, and the younger man recalled him with urgent proddings. Next, Oaive was taken to the hut where the sick child lay. There were several women there who gazed at her hopefully. Oaive tried to explain the herbs they should give to the child, but they only gaped, so she beckoned them to follow and went up to the hill-slopes. She was not absolutely certain she would find growing there anything she knew, but after a time she did. She and the women picked bunches of plants, and took them to the village to seethe in water over the smoky fire.

Oaive had started to identify the speech of the people.

It was the Old Tongue—the language in which the Book of Lore would be written. She saw she had never uttered it in the correct accent: she set herself to learn.

They had already adopted her into their colony as their healer and priestess. Presumably accustomed to dealing with simple facts simply, they ignored the strangeness of her arrival among them. She was useful, therefore acceptable.

In two days the sick child was well. By then, they had given Oaive a hut to live in, supplied her with food and a pot of the dark red metal in which to cook up her potions. She was the village witch. They were proud of her.

She did not know how long she would have to stay with them, earning their trust, before she could begin to question them. She needed their guidance to find what she sought, but she must move slowly. She had plenty of time—that was the irony. For, however long she lingered among them, she could return to that moment in the cedar tree when she had cast this sorcery, or to any other moment she chose—assuming that she could return at all. She never let herself doubt this, which was harder now.

Yet she felt a responsibility for the village, as she had felt responsible for her own people when she served the shrine. So she worked unremittingly for them. All day, women would slip in and out of her hut, to learn from her, watching the pot of herbs and her hands as intently as dogs looking for scraps. Against her going, Oaive began to teach her craft to the quickest of the little girls that came in with their mothers. It was best to instruct a child; the craft adhered to them better before their brains had been crammed with other things.

Oaive was trying to get the accent right. They would trust her the more if she sounded more like them.

Sunrise and sunset she climbed the path to the altar on the cliff, and said the Ritual. It gave her an odd sensation to speak those words on that windy headland so many years before they would come to be spoken. Truly, she was playing games with time.

Days went by like waves on the shore. Then a month had gone.

One morning she woke and the snow was down.

The land was a snapping white, and ice lay like green fish-scales at the edges of the sea.

No one went out much that day. They had stored food against the coming of the snow. They had a sort of huddling antipathy to it that kept them in groups. When night fell, they crowded into the Elder's hut. Somehow most of them squashed inside; even the dogs lurked by the door, growling softly. The villagers began to tell stories.

Finally, Oaive walked across to the Elder's hut, carefully stepped over all the dogs, and went among the people. They shoved each other aside to give her room close to the fire, where they could see her. Only the Elder obstinately forgot who she was.

It had occurred to her that she might glean some clue to the Relics from listening to the stories, but she did not. They told of the Cruel Winter King, and the Lord of the Fish, who sometimes sent his folk aground on the beach to feed the village, and sometimes did not, and of the wild demons of the sea. The tales were just like those the shrine villages would tell in the future.

Then a silence fell, and into the silence a man said: "A demon has come to live on the hill. It cries like a wolf, but the wolves never come this way in the cold."

Oaive's blood seemed to alter direction.

"Yes," another man said, "at moon-change I saw fire burning under the hill. When I went near, there was no fire but a blue light in a cave. Someone sat in the cave mouth and looked at me and never moved. His face was white as chalk. It was Lord Death himself, I believe."

Oaive drew in a breath.

Niwus had followed her.

She should have foreseen. Why should he wait? It would be easy for his magic to track her and come after. But then, why sit on the hill, and not seek her here? Perhaps he would, if she did not go to him. Perhaps he would punish these people who had sheltered her, as he had punished Grey's people. Yes. Niwus had meant the man to see him, meant her to hear of it. Niwus wanted her destruction now as badly as he wanted the Bone.

The entire crowd was looking at her. A woman said: "Is it true? Is it Death himself? Which of us has he come for?"

For me, Oaive thought bitterly. She said: "No, it is only a winter demon. He means you no harm, but I will go and make sure."

They murmured, pleased.

There seemed nothing else she could do. Having no longer any room for subtlety, she said directly: "To make me able to meet the demon, I will need your help. Are there any sacred things that you keep here?"

Again a murmur, this time puzzlement. She had anticipated a variety of reactions; that it should be only this disappointed and depressed her.

The Elder's son frowned. "No, lady. There is nothing."

"Not here? Near the altar?" She frowned. "I must know. I am your priestess."

"But, lady, we would say if we had anything you might find useful."

"A circle of metal," she said, testing them, "a shiny gem, a piece of bone."

Their eyes were beaded with light from the fire, intent and guileless. They would have helped her any way they could, so much was obvious.

The Relics had yet to be found in this era she had come to. She had travelled wrongly, her instinctive magic had misjudged. She must face Niwus alone after all.

I am stronger than I was. I must trust in *myself.*

"I will go tomorrow," she said.

A shadow darkened her heart.

There were clouds like sharks with open jaws in the sky that morning. At the door of Oaive's hut, one of the little girls was standing with a cake of bread and some heather beer for Oaive's excursion into the hills.

"Will you come home, or shall the demon kill you?" the child asked, harsh yet unmalicious as the ice ramming the bay.

"If he does, I will make the demon go with me to Death's place."

"Good," said the child with approval.

"Will you remember what I have taught you, if I don't return?"

"Yes. I remember. About the weeds and the bark in water and the sea-grasses and the words of the spells—and everything. I even know the special thing you say to the stone on the cliff. I have whispered it with you every day for days."

"When you are older, you will be the priestess, maybe."

"Maybe," said the child reflectively. "Then they will give me a hut, too."

Not many came out to see Oaive off. They thought it might be unlucky, and clearly were anxious and guilty that they had not been able to supply her with the mysterious items she had mentioned.

The snow was knee-deep, with a brittle, slippery top layer that broke. It was not pleasant walking on it. She thought: I left by this path once before, or rather, I *will* leave by this path in the future. Strange to admit I might die today, and yet still I shall live there, centuries ahead of myself. But it was not the hour for riddles.

When she was already on the lower slopes, she glanced over her shoulder, and saw the little girl running after her, sometimes falling over and not caring. Oaive stopped and waited.

The child scrambled up to her and stared at her.

"You won't come home. Say farewell to me."

Oaive turned colder than the snow had made her.

"How do you know this?"

"I have a feeling—as you said we should feel it, like tiny feet under the skin."

Evidently the child had witchcraft in her beyond Oaive's teaching. Oaive swallowed down a cindery taste, and smiled at her.

"Farewell, then, and guard your people when you are grown."

"I would rather travel beyond the mist as you have," said the child.

Oaive was startled. "Do you mean travel inland?"

"No. When you came here there was a dark place on the air. I was on the cliff, and I saw. The place was all mist, like a doorway out of a hut in leaf-fall. You jumped down from it, out of the mist. Then it closed up. It was funny," said the child. Her face screwed up, I and she giggled. She swung round and skidded off, and her hair burned like a dim smoky flame down the hill.

Her hair is like mine, Oaive thought suddenly. And for some reason that filled her with pride, and with anger. And then the answer struck her like a thunderbolt.

* * *

The sun was setting when she found the cave. The red light was going down behind the hills when a blue light ignited between them. That was where the cave was.

The way over the ice was easier here, the drifts packed hard. The cave mouth loomed up, a jagged rent of azure, coloring the snow. It looked empty. Then, as she came in close to the hill-wall, she saw a man seated on a rock just inside the entrance. It was Grey.

The cave behind him was all stippled and striped with the strange light. Grey's shining hair also appeared blue, and his skin and the whites of his eyes, and the gem-eyes in the mask of the wolf cloak. His teeth were like sapphires.

"Welcome, Oaive," Grey said to her. "You cost him some magic. You gave him a deal of trouble."

"You mean Niwus," she said.

"I mean Niwus. I mean he wishes you dead."

"Yes."

"All this—the pretty cave—all a lure to get you here."

"Yes. I know it."

"Then why come, Oaive? Why seek him out?"

"I have lost the Bone," she said. "Now both he and I must search, must we not? Perhaps we can search together, and fight for the prize later."

"He'd win that fight," Grey said. He looked at her contemptuously. "You're a poor sorceress, after all. I thought better of you. I thought you could master the magician, but you're only a silly little village conjurer off the coast, with a sleeveful of crackpot tricks to impress idiots."

His words were like lashes across her face. She winced at the bite of them. With a dry hot fury she said: "And you? What are you? His slave, half-beast, half-fool. You walk like a man, and carry a man's sword at your side, and you never ventured a blow of sword or deed for yourself.

Do you dare, in your weakness, to call me weak? In your rank stupidity do you *dare* to call me *silly?"*

He let out a bark of laughter and sprang off the rock. He came directly at her, and she thought he would hit her, and her hands were ready to hit him right back. Instead he took her by the shoulders. "Oaive," he said. *"Good,* Oaive." His face had altered. In an exhilarated whisper he said: "Beat him."

"Don't test me any more," she said. "You have no claim."

"Humbly your pardon, lady," he said, still delighted at her.

"Where is Niwus?"

"He is here. Are you in a hurry for death?"

"Where?"

"The cave. I am to take you to him. What will you do, Oaive, when he raises his hand to kill you?"

"Maybe I shall only die, and you will stay bound till eternity." She walked by him into the hollow hill. The cave widened upwards into a great vault.

"I am bringing her, my master," Grey called.

"Yes," someone answered ahead of them. "I heard you. Every dangerous word."

There was a fire at the cave's spine, an indigo fire that whined as it burned. Niwus sat there on a shelf of stone.

She hated his bloodless face, his hands, she hated the gold ring he wore, everything about him. The sinews in her legs turned to straw as she confronted him.

"So you lost the Bone among the copper-people," he said. "That was intelligent, Oaive."

"Listen," she said, "I travelled time. I can do it again. How long will you pursue me?"

"Forever. If necessary."

"I had best show you, in that case, where to seek the Bone."

"Show me."

"It is one of three Relics," she said quietly.

"Well? I am waiting."

"Grey," Oaive said, "draw the sword."

There was a brief silence. Grey said very lightly: "For what do I require a sword, under the protection of my kind master?"

"Grey," she said. The power stirred in her, her head sang. *"Do* it."

He put his hand on the hilt of the iron. It came from the scabbard, ringing softly.

"Witch," Niwus said, "remember me, and be careful."

"Niwus," she replied, "I am showing you how to seek the Bone. If you are too dull to see that, you are too dull to utter threats."

His terrifying eyes swivelled like a lizard's to Grey's sword. Oaive advanced across the cave. *Fire does not burn.* She moved straight through it, up to Niwus. She stretched out and, with a quick tug, pulled off the ring he wore.

"A Ring, a Jewel, a Bone," Oaive said. "This is the Ring. They will find it in the Blue Cave, tomorrow, or next year. The metal will tarnish and turn green with age. You will leave it here because you will die here." She pointed at the black wolf skin, at the gem-eyed wolf's head on Grey's shoulder. "One of those white stones is the Jewel; I wonder which? The copper-people will find that here also. It will lose its whiteness but not its brilliance. It will be knocked from its socket in the last struggle, when Grey kills you, Niwus, with his sword."

She detected the whine of the fire again. It had mouthed her feet and her skirt, and not even warmed them.

Niwus said: "Complex lies, witch. They don't disconcert me."

"I am glad," she said. "I don't intend your alarm.

Merely your death." She stared at Grey. "You reckon me a sorceress," she said. "Do what I say, and we shall see."

Grey's face was full of shadows and dread. He nodded. She could sense his heart pounding like her own.

"Grey," Niwus said, "obey me."

Oaive brought her hands abruptly on to Niwus' forehead, holding him tightly at the temples. "Grey," she cried, "finish it now!"

Instantly Niwus thrashed to get loose. He writhed and the world writhed. The cave groaned, and particles of rock shot from walls and roof.

Niwus was speaking the word that twisted shape and form.

Grey was already running forward. Midway, the force of the word caught him. He spun aside, shouting out.

A wolf landed at the brink of the fire; its shadow danced behind it. Its irises were pale blank slits, no reasoning left.

When Grey is wolf, his brain is nearly a wolf's brain.

The wolf edged around the fire. Its shadow went too, emphasizing what it did. It crouched, and the hide slid over its ribs as it gathered air into itself. Next second it exploded into a massive leap to clear the flames and reach her throat.

Oaive seemed to catch the moment like a white-cold flame between her fingers. She saw the wolf suspended in space, straining at her. She somehow held it back, and held Niwus as frantically. Niwus' flesh was like frozen clay, dead stuff already. When he had lent Grey his magic so long before, Grey had turned himself from man to animal. That single time he had acted like man not wolf. And on the ship he had said: *I will tell you my name. One day I may need you to call me by that name.*

Oaive strove to release herself. It was a clamor, an

agony, like dying or being born. Then the magic came and brimmed her over.

Niwus was small. He had no strength, she could subdue him easily. The power in her sizzled, flared.

"Cyrdin," she said, "Cyrdin, you are a man. Believe what I say."

The wolf dropped down, its feet scattering the blue fire. It yelped.

"Cyrdin, men cannot be cursed into wolves."

The wolf shook itself; it tried to rear up on its hind limbs. It whimpered from the pit of its lungs.

"Man, not beast, Cyrdin."

The power was suddenly so huge she felt herself dissolving in it. Niwus muttered magics, but the power deflected them, scorched them.

"Cyrdin. *Man.* Not *wolf.*"

She knew she had won.

It was like a cloud-burst. The power flooded from her, enveloping everything.

Niwus was floundering in her grip, a swimmer drowning in heavy seas.

Grey was across the fire. He was a man. He jumped forward, his arm lifted. The sword dazzled like stars. Oaive's hands let go of Niwus as the sword cleaved through him.

Oaive screamed. She fell backwards.

The pain was worse than she could imagine. It swallowed her whole side, beginning at the roots of her fingers.

In striking Niwus dead, the sword had slashed off the tip of her right forefinger. As she had known it must. She had refound the Bone; later the copper-people would also find it, with the other Relics in the cave. The Bone was hers. It had always been.

* * *

The body of Niwus crumbled away into a heap like rough flour. Even the bones crumbled. It had no odor. Of course, the flesh of Niwus had been dead six years. Presently, it was indistinguishable from the powdery floor of the cave.

Oaive sat against the wall and watched this happen, while Grey bound her hand and stopped it bleeding.

Grey's head was bowed. His face was cold and locked with shame. When he had finished, he sat beside her in the blue firelight. The wolf head of his cloak winked; its left eye was gone.

"I never dreamed it could be so simple," he said. "I always concluded it would take a blast from hell itself to be rid of him. He clung on my back so long, I thought I couldn't shake him off. It was so simple. I feel I should have guessed and killed him years ago, without your help. Then this would not have happened to you."

"You were too much his slave to do it alone," she said. "I was nearly that too. You had the right of it. I must have faith in myself but you also must have faith in yourself. You taught me my part. I taught you yours."

"Your hand—"

"My hand will heal."

"Granted. Thus, what now?"

"I wonder," she said. She gazed about her. She was calm, melancholy. "I have been wondering for some while. After we leave this place, the copper-people will come, probably in the thaw. They will take the Ring and the Jewel and the Bone from the dust, and venerate them as mystic symbols—not least because I spoke of them before I abandoned the village. The people will say I conquered the demon, but they understand so little about me, less about the demon, that they won't be able to clothe the facts in satisfactory myth. The history of the Relics will be forgotten. Sometime they will build the shrine about their altar. The priestess of the shrine will be the child to whom I passed on my healer's knowledge. Customs will grow up around the shrine, belief and magic, and the seeds of power. Eventually I shall be born, far in the future, and become one of that order, unaware that I began it."

"So it was not Niwus' game we played," he said. "Do you suppose God is playing with us? Some god or other?"

"Perhaps," she murmured, "perhaps not."

"But is it done?"

"No," she said.

"I surmised it was not."

"There is still the future," she said. "Even though Niwus died here in the past, in the future he has yet to be. The wandering spirit will enter the priest's body, he will force you into bondage, he will curse your house. You will kill your father and run with the wolf pack. Then Niwus will send you to steal the Bone. With his sorcerous gift, he always sensed the Bone would destroy him, and, in trying to avoid destruction, he caused it.

"But consider, the three of *us* have given the Relics to this people. It will all begin once more. In the future you will thieve the Bone, and I will go after you. I shall confront Niwus and travel the Time Road, then we will fight him again in this cave—and again the Ring, the Jewel, the Bone will be left in the dust for the people to adopt. It is endless, Grey. We are caught on a wheel of time, turning forever."

She held her bound hand before her. "Maybe we have come this way before, and acted out these things before, and sat here afterwards to talk of them. Except that now I see a remedy, a method of breaking the circle. Or have I tried to break it before, and failed? Or have I not dared to try? Maybe I, or you, or both of us were too afraid to change so much. For to break the pattern will be to alter both our lives."

He said, glancing at her: "You had better say it all."

"I had better. Let me tell you first the alternative. The people in this earlier world are kind and innocent. We could remain here."

He took her sound hand in his.

"One with one," he said.

"Yes. One with one, you and I. No other way."

"That's as I see it," he said.

They looked at each other. She said: "I hazard that is what we did before. Possibly we journeyed inland, across the hills—I think we never saw the building of the shrine. But I don't remember that we were happy. We were far from our own folk; guilt and memory came in between—and horror at what lay ahead, the next turn of the wheel when it was all to be done again.... I will tell you the rest. I have travelled time. I can go forward. I can go to the fallen mountain on the night when the hermit-priest died there. I can wait for the boy who is to be Grey. I can prevent you from speaking the spells of cadamancy. I can stop you calling the spirit of Niwus into the priest's body. You were very young then; I will comfort you and make you obey me."

"Then none of this will happen—will have happened."

"None of it. We shall be free of the trap."

"I shall grow up," he exclaimed, "with a smattering of sorcery, to be a nobleman's son. I shall live well in the towered house above the river villages. My father will hunt and laugh, my mother will make tapestries at her loom—there will be no wolves in the forest, no murder, no black pelt—" Grey's facc was lit, his eyes glittered. Then the inner lamp went out in them. "And I shall never steal the Bone for Niwus, I shall never come near the shrine by the sea. We will never meet, Oaive."

"More than that," she said, "we will never leave in this cave a Ring, a Jewel and a piece of Bone, since we shall never have come here. *There will be no Relics.* Neither shall I ever have stayed among the copper-people to teach them healing or prayer. There will be no shrine, no Ritual. No priestess. In my future, what shall *I* be?"

"Oaive," he said, "it is too much. Everything on my side, and nothing for you. We will stay where we are. For this turn of the wheel, and for all its turns."

She smiled. "I saw your face. I saw the light in it. If I ignored your happiness last time, I cannot any longer." She let go of his hand. Her fingers raked in the dust, and closed. She drew the power up inside her like a wave. "Farewell, Grey."

It was swift now. The black mist came swirling in and lifted her away into itself. Faint as the sea behind her, she heard him call out her name.

It was not hard to locate that night. The misery and hurt of it marked it out.

She came to the hermitage on the fallen mountain, and the pines soughed below in the wind. She sat by the dead priest till the sun rose and the boy came in at the door. His hair was grey, and he stood there staring at her.

"Don't be afraid," she said. "He has died, but I will help you. I promise."

7. Sea Blue

THE SUMMER SEA WAS WIDE and blue as the great sail of sky rigged over it, and on the cliff top above the bay there were garlands of flowers laid out on the ancient altar.

Three girls sat on the cliff, laughing together, and arranging herbs to dry in the sun. One had a heap of shells in her lap. Her hair was a smoky, ashen bronze, and she held it from her face with one hand as she examined the shells and placed them in a basket. Her name was Oaive, a name like the sound of the sea. She was seventeen and, like her two friends, she was a witch.

You never knew how many would be born with this natural witch-power, but generally there were two or three naturals in each generation. They were long-lived; Oaive's tutor was in her nineties and still thriving. Generally the older adepts taught the younger, but occasionally it was the other way about, when some new psychic ability manifested itself in a younger one. Often it was a woman's daughter who would inherit her own power, for the people had no lore which said a sorceress must live separately and not marry.

Though Oaive's mother had not been a witch, they had been close. The mother was proud that her child would be a healer and spell-maker for the fisher-folk and the shepherds and hunters on the hills. After her mother's death, Oaive had been sad a long while, but with the coming of summer her sorrow eased.

Suddenly the oldest of the laughing girls jumped up and pointed down the cliff path.

"Someone is coming from the village. A stranger."

"Oh, you are always seeing things. It's probably only a stray dog."

"No, it is an old man."

Oaive and the other girl got up to look too.

"It never is an old man, but a young one."

"He must have come hill-over," said the oldest girl to Oaive. "Hill-over" meant the unknown terrain inland, where none of them had ever ventured.

The three young witches stood with the sun behind them, and waited for the stranger. He strode right up to them.

The witches looked at him favorably. Though his hair was shining grey, he was young and well dressed. The blue cloak made his eyes seem blue. He smiled, and his teeth were white as the wave-crests out on the ocean.

"Good day," he said. "Will you tell me where I might find your sorceress?"

"She is here," said the oldest girl.

"And here," said the other.

"Also here," added Oaive. "As you note, we are not short of witches."

The man moved around to get the sun out of his eyes. His face changed subtly. He looked at Oaive. "Yes," he said, "you are the one."

Oaive gazed back at him. It was strange. She seemed

to know him, and he to know her, though they had never met.

"I? What have I done?"

"No," he said, "surely not you. You lack the years. Did your mother have witch-power too?"

"No," said Oaive, "I am the first in my family."

"My mother was a healer," burst out the youngest girl, "and her mother, and— "

But the oldest girl grasped her arm. "I am supposing we are wanted somewhere for some reason," she said, and, nodding to Oaive, she yanked the youngest off down the path.

The grey-haired man grinned. He said: "I have come a distance and a half to find one like you, with just such hair."

"Why?"

"Because when I was a child, one like you came into my life and kept me from a mistake so bad that when I remember it now my blood rattles."

"What mistake?" she asked. It was so odd, she felt on the verge of recollecting this story she could not conceivably know.

"It was to do with cadamancy, the summoning of a spirit. She stopped me before I opened that dark and dangerous gate. Or was it you stopped me?"

Oaive laughed. She liked him. "Not I."

"Well then. We'll put that aside. I am something of a magic-worker too, which is how I found you."

"I don't understand. I also can find things and people—but you must have some part of them by which to track—a lock of hair, or a piece of their clothing."

"Ah. I had something. Something you gave me—or the woman, whoever she was. It led me to you. So how do you account for that?"

"Show it to me," she said.

He opened his hand. There on his palm lay a smooth little bit of bone.

"That is not mine," Oaive said, astonished. "It's a finger bone, and see—" She held out her hands, both whole.

He said: "You, or she, left it in the priest's hall, on the altar there. It was wrapped in a cloth. She spoke some word over it, I think to preserve it, as if she expected it might vanish out of place and time. To me she said: 'Do not look at it now, but when six years have passed, look at it then, if you want, and afterwards seek me with it, if you wish.' I am glad I did."

"I am glad," said Oaive.

"What is your name?" he asked her.

"Oaive. And do they call you 'Grey'?"

"A few call me Grey, but my name is Cyrdin. How long must I court you?"

"Not long," she answered, "not very long."